WESTING

Adam Ahlbrandt

WESTING

Cover Design and Story Copyright © 2024 by Adam Ahlbrandt

All rights reserved. No part of this book may be reproduced or transmitted in any form or by any means without written permission from the author.

DEDICATION

I would like to dedicate this work to everyone who stood by me through thick and thin; my friends Kacie, James and Anthony who've seen my highs and lows. To my father, who still cuts his neighbors lawns and is kind to absolutely everyone. To my wife Savannah for being a daily inspiration and my drive-in movie date. To my family, with whom I can finally share some of my works; sorry that it's taken so long. Zoe', Lily, Scarlett, Ivy and Von; I live to see you all prosper and grow and am so astonished by everything you've all become. I hope you enjoy this story and it reminds all of you, no matter what; I love you.

Never give up.

TABLE OF CONTENTS

Chapter One: A beaten man, not a broken man.11
Chapter Two: The first night on the job............57
Chapter Three: A new story. 110
Chapter Four: The secrets of Westing............203
Chapter Five: Life imitates art. 283
Chapter Six: No one knows what waits for them at the end of the road..375
Afterwards..387

There was no way Alison could move past it to reach the stairwell and get to the first floor, she was cornered by it; trapped. "Help me!!!" Alison screamed out in desperation to the night watchman and custodian who were also working the late shift, playing cards at the watchman's desk downstairs in the building's lobby. Immediately she could hear them come running from the floor below but it was already too late.

Its eyes were upon her.

The immolation consumed Alison Hawley in a flash and by the time the two men reached her on the second floor, she was already completely ablaze.

No one could ever truly explain what had happened, sure it'd been an early summer day and the library

WESTING

did tend to get rather hot; it was after all a very old building with an inadequate cooling system. Some speculation was given to the theory that the clothing the elderly librarian Alison Hawley had been wearing was made from combustible material but certainly that wouldn't account for the thoroughness of her burns or the inexplicable localization of the blaze itself. Nor did it clear up the fact that Alison Hawley had been wearing the exact same outfit daily for the better part of thirty years to that very same library.

The custodian and night watchman both had also seen something during the event. Something neither one of them detailed to the sheriff when he took their statements. Something that had made both men tender their resignations. When they initially saw Alison Hawley engulfed in the blaze there had been someone there with her.

Someone holding her in the flames.

CHAPTER ONE: A BEATEN MAN, NOT A BROKEN MAN.

It was the fall of 1974 and Gary Wettle had just applied for the night custodian/watchman position at the library in the rural town of Westing Pennsylvania. Being well read, tall at over six foot and physically capable he assumed would make an ideal candidate. Sure his once dark brown hair had begun to grey at the temples but he was still a specimen and an educated one at that. He'd seen an add in the help wanted section of his local newspaper, Gary

WESTING

only bought the papers for the help wanted
advertisements at that point in his life.

He didn't read the current events portion of the
paper anymore, most of it was trash gossip the way
Gary saw it and poorly written to boot. It also
reminded him of different times in his life he'd rather
not dredge up. If Gary had looked on the front page
he would have seen the news and put two and two
together right then and there about why the position
was available, like most people outside of Westing
did. All Gary had seen was the want ad and decided
excitedly to apply.

The old library was one of the few remaining
buildings in Westing that still stood from prior to the
civil war. Almost the entirety of the other original
homesteads were destroyed by fire, supposedly by
confederate looters fleeing the great battle of

Gettysburg. There were many town residents who doubted that theory as the journey to get to Westing at that point in it's history wasn't easy, it was a town with no roads leading into or out of it save one. Westing was also northwest of the battle, with all of the confederate army observed to have been fleeing directly south.

Some blamed the mining company that moved in immediately after and bought up all the land, others said that the town was cursed. Gary was more prone to believe that a greedy mining group was responsible as it had been his experience that there wasn't anything people wouldn't do for money. Anything. Swallow their pride, morals, throw away their friends, family and lovers, commit robbery, extortion, murder… You name it, for cold hard cash it was on the menu.

WESTING

The library itself had been a church at it's construction and it's architecture still held some semblance of that history, however folks around Westing were poor and the baskets of any preachers who'd tried their luck at selling the gospels there were always empty. The building was vacant for many years after the religious fervor of Westing's founders had dried up, until the town decided to intercede on behalf of the decaying property. Seeing of course the benefits of such a grand building and pointing to it having been built upon the tenant that it be shared by all the settlers of Westing, the officials turned it into a public project after the procurement of a federal grant.

Free land is free land and everyone loves free, especially when it's the government. As soon as the town repossessed the building it was converted to the library and overseen by its first librarian who had once seemed to have a bright future, Alison Hawley. The same Alison Hawley who had mysteriously burst

Sarah and Caleb were his strength when times were darkest.

After the divorce Gary had worked dead end jobs wherever he could to make enough to afford his rattrap apartment, even at that he hadn't been very successful. Gary had to constantly borrow money from his father to make up the difference almost every month. His father was the best man he'd ever known. A man who'd married the wrong woman in his youth but hadn't let her bitterness spoil him. Even after Gary's mother had left them, taking as much of his father's savings as she could; trying to make their lives as miserable as her own. Gary's father still was the kindest, most honest person Gary had ever known. He still cut his elderly neighbors lawns and made sure they all were looked after, even in his old age of 72.

WESTING

Gary hadn't followed in his father's footsteps. He had admittedly made countless bad decisions in his life. There had been a time in his youth where it seemed that fortune might smile on Gary and his creative endeavors but that time was now a distant memory. No one read his stories anymore. His agent had stopped returning his calls and no publishing house would touch him.

He'd squandered his chances and now Gary found himself fighting to rebuild his tarnished image, he even considered using a different name but his father told him he thought he shouldn't. The old man had told Gary it was time to stop running away from his name or his problems. So Gary decided he would keep it. Part of making amends is taking responsibility. Being a better person means owning up to your bad choices. Trying to do better as a person is hard because it means accepting that you've been the problem. These truths he knew all too well.

Gary knew he'd been the problem. No doubt about it. He was trying his hardest to make better choices and be honest with everyone. It wasn't easy but nothing would stop him. Nothing would stop him from doing better by his children, or his father; or himself. Nothing would stop Gary from sitting at his typewriter every day and banging away on the keys until the ink ribbon ran dry or he forced himself into bed. Despite everything Gary still had hope in his heart that maybe, one day, he'd get lucky and write something people cared about as much as he did.

Because he did care.

Even after all the failures and shame.

WESTING

One of his favorite things to dream of was making everything better somehow, scoring big and turning everything around. Believing he still had a chance to. A focused mind can achieve goals most people think are unobtainable because they look at them in totality instead of one step at a time. It was one of the self-help mantras that rang truest to him. Gary's childhood neighbor had been an army veteran who always repeated the saying: "Every hole gets dug one shovelful at a time." It was a mentality that Gary was embracing.

Gary spent every free moment with a pot of coffee and his dreams, pouring them both out until it was time to work or sleep or see his children whom he loved so very dearly. He picked up a thesaurus or a dictionary almost as often as he took breath into his lungs, dreaming of the greatest writers and how often it's not just that they have a robust vocabulary;

it's that they have a knowledge of when to keep things simple. They also all have a story worth telling.

Still, Gary was sure every writer worth their words poured through both books for just the right way to phrase something beautifully. That was a large part of what made the job at the library so appealing to him. Even though Gary had become someone who didn't write about beautiful things, he still liked to paint the details into his stories ornately with his vast knowledge of semantics.

Gary wrote primarily morbid tales. Horror stories and dark mysteries. Stories his family disapproved of. Looking back of course they were over the line. Garbage. Smut. Not anything to take pride in. Things that Gary had grown to feel ashamed of. His ex wife had threatened to use them against him in court

WESTING

unless he acquiesced to her demands in the divorce. So he had and lost everything in the process. Everything but two days with his children every other weekend, an offer he wouldn't take up for a few years as Gary Wettle hit bottom and his home became the street.

Life on the street seemed like it was both easier and worse than Gary imagined. He was able to drink away most of his troubles for a time, continuing to travel further down a dark path in his work and his life. That had changed when Gary decided to do two tabs of LSD by himself, alone around his campfire.

He'd dropped a single tab three nights previously and it'd made the colors dance out of the fire into beautiful mirages before his eyes, giving him wonderful thoughts of happiness and hope, something he desperately desired. He'd watched the birth of the sun and wrote poems about true love that had brought him to tears of joy. And so Gary had decided to try it again, this time with what he assumed would only be a slightly larger dose.

The experience began pleasantly enough; Gary had been sitting peacefully admiring the campfire, listening to the night's low hum of crickets and the slight rustling of the leaves from the night's breeze. He imagined time slowing down and that he could distinguish the sound of every individual chirp of the cricket's wings. The colors of the forest night were electric, neon hues of turquoise and evergreen surrounded Gary as he sat in front of his fire. No longer was he unable to see in the darkness, now Gary could make out great details where once was pitch black. Gary was overwhelmed by his newfound vision of the nighttime forest and decided to look back into his fire. Only now the fire seemed to be a living thing within which he was able to see visions of his own life up to that point.

WESTING

At first the visions were cheerful and sentimental but as Gary looked deeper into it's depths he began to see reminders of all of his wrongs and transgressions. Gary tried to look away up into the sky overhead which had turned into a beautiful show of spectral lights, although that too quickly faded to darkness leaving Gary with no other place but the fire to look.

Thankfully the fire had ceased being anything more than that. Just a burning pile of sticks and logs. After staring into the flames for what felt an eternity the night fell hushed, so much so that Gary could hear his own heartbeat thundering through his veins. It felt as though there was something approaching from somewhere unseen around him in the darkness, he knew he couldn't panic and kept telling himself it was only the drugs making him paranoid.

That didn't stop his terror.

As he slowly surveyed the darkness around his campfire Gary could make out something he hoped wasn't real, the faintest glimmer of a sea of eyes surrounding him. Endless points of unblinking eyes glaring back from the endless dark, hovering just at the very edge of the firelight's illumination. Gary watched in horror as out of nowhere his blazing fire suddenly went out, as if someone had dumped a lump of soot into it.

Gary didn't dare to get up to try to stoke the embers back to life, he felt the drugs kicking in hard and he knew he shouldn't move for any reason at all. It was just a bad trip Gary kept assuring himself, everything was ok he'd just taken too much and would have to ride it out. He also couldn't see any smoldering coals left on the ground in front of him where they should have been, try as hard as he might.

"It's only the drugs. It's only the drugs. I'm just tripping and I need to relax." Struggling to keep calm Gary couldn't shake the terrible feeling that he wasn't alone in the forest that night, tripping or not; not far away in the pitch black he could hear someone else breathing. A forest no one else on earth should have been in.

The crickets had long since gone silent and whatever breeze there had been stilled until Gary couldn't hear even the rustling of a single leaf in the surrounding trees. He'd been deep in the middle of the woods, woods that he knew would be easy to get lost in if you wandered off during the night, especially on hard psychotropic drugs. The breathing remained.

"Don't panic. It's just the drugs. Get ahold of yourself." Gary knew he couldn't give into the fear, there was too much that could go wrong in the wilderness surrounding his campsite. He'd picked it because he knew the owner of the property, they'd been friends prior to his divorce; he wasn't all together sure where they stood after. It was an undeveloped lot of dense forest stretching for miles in all directions and Gary knew no one would bother him there.

Not the owner who rarely if ever went to the property, as it was simply his family's estate and the cabin they had on it was miles away on the other side. It was also in such a remote part of the Pennsylvania backwoods that very few people ever even drove within a hundred miles of it. Gary also

WESTING

knew that because he was so remote it could be years before anyone came looking in this part of the property if he were to get lost.

Gary decided that it was imperative to sit still.

Gary tried to look back up at the moon and stars through the trees overhead to pass the time but now he couldn't even make those out. It was nothing but pitch-blackness all around him. A smell festered in the dark, an overwhelming rancid stench of burnt and decayed cadaverous rot. Gary began wondering if he'd somehow accidentally taken too much LSD and had gone blind. He didn't exactly trust the dealer he'd bought it off of, Gary's mind raced with conspiracies and worse case scenarios. Maybe he'd taken an overdose without even knowing? Maybe the dealer had made a terrible mistake and given him too much or maybe the drugs were laced with something else? All he knew was he couldn't see anything and the pungency of the stench was overwhelming him.

Gary sat as still as he could trying to calm himself down and not freak out, when he remembered he had a book of matches in his pocket. After fumbling around with his arms for a time trying to coordinate them to move, he discovered they had lost a sense of normal functioning; Gary was finally able to locate the matches and strike one with more than a little clumsiness. It's flint struck barely a few feet in front of his face and the antimony trisulfide and potassium chlorate ignited.

Scht…

Gary had not gone blind after all, although in that

WESTING

moment he wished that he had.

What the match illuminated was a wall of twisted and unspeakable faces peering back at him from the darkness on all sides. A swarm of faces with unblinking eyes. Staring at him like starved animals everywhere around him in the dark. He dropped the match the moment his vision registered the image in his mind, leaving Gary to spend the rest of the night huddling in the infested darkness too crippled with fear to move. The sounds of wheezing breath being drawn surrounding him.

Slowly, after what felt like forever, the smell went away, although Gary couldn't stop smelling it for weeks after. Then the sounds of the crickets returned and Gary was able to force himself to open his eyes and look up to see the predawn sky overhead. He was alone and unharmed.

His relief was short lived, as Gary realized that he wasn't sitting in front of his fire any longer; nor was his car or the neglected backwoods dirt road he'd driven in on anywhere within his sight. Gary was alone in the middle of the deep forest, with no sense whatsoever of where he was or which direction he should take to get back to civilization. He was lost, with no good options to get himself out of the very real possibility of dying. It was just as he'd feared, he must have panicked and fled in the night under the influence of the hallucinogens. Gary by no means felt any less delirious as his coordination and normal perception hadn't returned to him completely yet, however he was cognitive enough to know he was completely lost.

Before he knew it hours had passed, the sun had fully rose and begun to hang low in the sky. It seemed to happen so fast Gary had thought it only took a few seconds. As if time had been sped up and flown by. His perception seemed to be fully returned to normal after that shift but his situation and outlook remained dire. Even though Gary had regained control over himself and his perception, he couldn't be sure of it or of anything for that matter. Nothing seemed real, it was as if the forest was still filled with hidden lurkers harboring only sadistic intent, watching him every moment; some even very close by. Gary tried not to think of the hallucination of the faces but couldn't help it. He felt the same terror from the night before, an oppressive weight of primal fear. He tried to focus on getting his situation under control, telling himself to not let the fear win.

Gary looked for any signs of life or hints at which direction he should head in and couldn't come up with any idea as to where he exactly was. He knew which way the sun was setting and tried to move in the opposite direction, hypothesizing how he most likely had traveled the night before; knowing full well he had no real bearing on his course.

Gary walked through the desolate forest until the sun had set far enough that walking any further was impossible in the darkened thicket and so, dejectedly; Gary set about making himself a fire and collecting wood for the night. His pants were in tatters by that point from the dense brambles he'd trekked through all day so he imagined a fire would be important. The evening wasn't particularly cold but Gary was still more than a little afraid of his horrifying trip from the night before and hoped that a fire might also help calm him. He certainly had no intention of spending the evening alone and lost in the darkened forest without it. Gary no longer felt any effects of the drug in his system and in spite of his apprehension, after a few hours of tending the fire without incident he relaxed, giving into his exhaustion and fell fast asleep by it's warmth.

WESTING

Gary awoke sometime in the middle of the night, his fire smoldering a few feet in front of him. After piling a few sticks on it and blowing on the embers Gary was able to get it going again. He was in luck as there was a downed tree he'd spotted in the setting sunlight that was dry and rotten. It sat a few yards away from where Gary made his campfire and he was able to harvest more than enough wood from it to last through the night. After building the fire back up as large as he thought was safe, Gary sunk back down next to it and drifted back off into sleep.

When Gary awoke he was sitting in his chair at his original campfire, just a few yards from his car. Sure his pants were tattered in exactly the same fashion as he remembered from the day he'd just spent "lost" in the woods but Gary quickly convinced himself it was all one long trip and that he'd never left. That is until he drove into town and saw the date on a paper. Gary had indeed been somewhere he couldn't account for, for the span of an entire 24 hours.

That night having nowhere else to crash Gary again returned to the camp site but instead of making a fire he decided to simply go to sleep in the backseat of his car. Gary didn't dally by watching the sun set as was his usual custom, as soon as he parked he climbed into his backseat and locked his doors. He'd picked up a bottle of whiskey earlier in the day that he absolutely demolished, drunkenly hunkered away in his cramped cab. Gary fell almost immediately into a deep, comfortable sleep.

That night Gary was startled awake to the sound of someone aggressively trying his locked door handle from the driver's side of his car. Gary called out that he had a gun, which was a lie; when the sound abruptly stopped. Gary waited, expecting to hear the sounds of someone running away into the night.

WESTING

There was nothing.

Gary made the decision to flee. He got into the front seat, turned the engine on, wiped his windshield off so he could see through the condensation, flashed on the car's high beams and peeled out. There was no one in sight as Gary pulled out of the woods at top speed, something for which Gary was extremely grateful; although he couldn't rationally explain to himself how the person had managed to escape into the forest without making any sound.

Gary drove to the nearest hotel and parked in the lot to sleep there for the remainder of the evening. Reluctantly he again crawled into the backseat after checking all the door locks anew and was about to tuck back in, already resigned to the fact that he most likely wouldn't sleep a wink; when Gary saw something that sunk his heart into his stomach.

The glass that had been just above his head in the backseat window had a hand print shaped patch of condensation wiped clean from outside.

Whoever had tried his door had been watching him sleep.

The experience had shocked him and in many ways helped him see what was really his path in life.

He'd quit the bottle.

WESTING

He got two jobs and a crappy apartment.

It wasn't long after that Gary got himself back on his feet he and he was again able to get together with his children. They were still happy to see him and the trio tried to make the best of it. Cramming into his tiny one bedroom, eating better than Gary would for the next two weeks, going to the cinema to see the old double feature matinees.

Truth be told even though it wasn't the easiest life Gary enjoyed it tremendously and looked on the best side of things whenever possible. Trying to look at the bright spots instead of focusing on how much had gone wrong for him really did help Gary redefine himself as a new man. To great consequence as a writer he reminded himself constantly that no matter what, he could always dream and in doing so, escape.

"One word at a time, write your ticket." Gary figured he could also use his failures to make his life better and work more truthful, to show he'd indeed learned a lesson to the people who mattered in his life. To his children. To his father. To the people he'd wronged and himself.

Gary had a newfound happiness and appreciation of life, he believed things were going to get good again and that all he needed to do was enjoy it. "Do your work, hard work pays off." As Gary would constantly remind himself. Self-help really had struck a nerve in Gary Wettle, it was simply relatable to him. You either let fear or unhealthy vices cripple you or you believed in yourself and work hard to make your dreams come true. Gary was excited about the prospects of a new job, even if he knew it might be hard. It was just another step down the right path in his mind.

WESTING

The library itself was beautiful in a gothic sort of way, standing imposingly alone on the apex of the last ridge in the rural town of Westing. A lonely crest mostly covered by conifer forests, which butted up against the neighboring county line. Gary had caught a glimpse of it on his way in for the interview and again driving back out. He decided that no other standing building in Westing he'd seen had such fine masonry or woodwork as the old library, even the courthouse. Mostly all other surviving structures in Westing at that point had been built cheaply in the late 1800's, when the coal mine first opened. Properties thrown up to house and serve the influx of workers the mine brought with it to the tiny backwoods town.

For a time the town of Westing prospered while the mine flourished but that time dried up soon enough when several parts of the coal vein were discovered to travel under the town proper.

Then of course there was the collapse.

People who didn't live in Westing only heard the stories of the horrific cave in, mostly it was ignored in the papers because of how remote the town was. Gary hadn't grown up in Westing. He didn't know much about it's less than favorable reputation, other than it wasn't where nice people were looking to live or vacation.

Gary had moved from his boyhood hometown when the divorce finally came down but not to Westing. Truthfully Westing was known as the place you either were born into or ended up when you were down and out. Junkies from other towns, hillbillies and old folks still collecting their settlement from the

WESTING

mine catastrophe made up the majority of the population that inhabited Westing in the fall of 1974. Every other building on Main Street at that point was boarded up and most of the houses were deserted, the town had dried up and died sometime in the early 60's when the coal mine shut it's doors and sealed off the by that point unstable shaft.

Gary heard about the collapse from a gas station attendant who he had asked for directions on his way to the interview. The old man's face bore the weight of the grim tale as he told it and Gary had tipped him, then left in silence afterwards. He'd thought that must have been the worst way to go, to have had to wait in total suffocating darkness knowing you'll never see the light of day again. Each breath you took drawing you closer to your last. The chances of escape or salvation dwindling by the second.

Thirty-two men had lost their lives one day in late August 1962 when their tunnel caved in. Slowly asphyxiating to death, unable to be reached because of depth and impenetrable surrounding rock wall; alone in the cut off shaft. Most of the bodies were never recovered.

Westing had a long history of misfortunes, the tunnel collapse being the most prominent and the main reason behind the mine finally closing it's doors, although the profitability of Westing's coal vein had plummeted by that time under the newly implemented federal restrictions. There had also been a rash of unexplained disappearances over the years, in addition to several unexplained fires prior to the mine collapse in Westing.

When there is money coming in people tend to stick around.

WESTING

The fires plagued many of the original buildings over the years and were never solved. Some said it was copycats or descendants of the confederate arsonists, or as most believed a lone person; likely a sick degenerate who was unable to stop their compulsions. Arson was indeed suspected in many of the cases but nothing was ever officially proven to be the cause.

In fact most of Westing's history was equally as bleak. People tended to live short and often terrible lives there and many met their ends in brutal or suspicious fashion. The more Gary looked into the run down mountain town, the more sordid history he discovered.

It was one of the central reasons Gary moved there.

He intended to base his newest novel on the grisly little mountain settlement, which had grown into a place of lore amongst the inhabitants of the neighboring burrows. However morbid it might seem to many, all of Westing's horrific past made the town that much more alluring to Gary. It's terrible history rich fodder for his creative ambitions. Not unlike his own past, Gary was looking at the town's history as a source of inspiration.

Why shouldn't he try and make the best of all of it he thought?

Not to mention the idea of putting away books sure sounded better than cutting lawns or humping loads of bricks all day long which had been his only real paying occupations ever since the divorce. His ex-wife's family had fired him from his once hated job of warehouse manager, a position which had since

WESTING

seemed more like cake-work over the back breaking labor he'd had to take on since. They'd done it two days after Christmas. He was homeless by New Year's.

In fact Gary loved the notion of burrowing himself away in the town of Westing, far from the judging, mocking eyes of everyone who'd known him. Where he wouldn't be a walking joke. Westing was perfect for that. The locals didn't seem to want anything to do with anyone not from there. In fact, his landlord Mrs. Sullivan explained that folks kept to themselves in the town and that new residents were generally distrusted on account of the rash of bad run-ins with junkies and cons. She'd also promptly demanded his security deposit, first and last months rent and told him she had a no drugs or adult company policy; his children would be permissible as long as there wasn't any loud noise.

Gary was nervous that she would ask for references but she didn't seem to care anything about who he was or where he was from as soon as he produced the cash and that was perfectly fine to Gary. No questions asked. He left her house keys in hand.

Living in a place where he was just an old man with no attachments to anyone was exactly what Gary had been longing for ever since his ex-wife had kicked him out of their home on that frosty day in December. Without a doubt it'd been his fault, all the drinking and cavorting hadn't been the right way to honor their marriage. She'd left him penniless and on the street. That time was the hardest, even his father had turned him away, knowing first hand that Gary'd been throwing his life away down the gutter.

However deeply Gary wished he could say it wasn't true, he knew that it was. He'd found a comfortable low to drift away on. Let years slip by. Good years. Done a lot of harm to his children's lives and hearts, abandoning them as he did. Not to mention his ex-wife and father. All the irreparable harm he'd done to their hearts, it made him consider the easy way out. But the easy way out would only hurt them more and it was a sad excuse for trying to put things right. Gary preferred to not give excuses to himself anymore, excuses were the permissions he'd used to enable his misery in the first place.

It had been tough to live in the back seat of his car, scrounging for work just to be able to afford a tiny room in a boarding house but he'd done it. Gary had quit the bottle for good. Fought his way back into his children's lives and into regular showers and meals. It hadn't been easy but Gary was a fighter, a survivor. Through it all he'd never given up hope. Sure there had been dark moments but in the end he knew in his heart he couldn't let his children or his father down, he loved them too much.

Gary remained a dreamer and a dreamer can always dream. When you've got a dream anything is possible, especially if you believe in it. Gary believed in his dreams. Everyday he was working his hardest to make them come true.

CHAPTER TWO: THE FIRST NIGHT ON THE JOB.

Gary arrived at the grand if not imposing building early, eager to make a good impression on his new boss Mrs. Culligan; a stern second generation Irish woman who'd also recently moved up from overnight clerk and been given the task of head librarian. She'd held her previous position under the past librarian Alison Hawley for almost twenty years. The old custodian and watchmen had all quit upon the prior librarian's departure as far as Gary was aware and both positions had been combined into one. At that point Gary Wettle was completely oblivious to the bizarre and nightmarish circumstances of Alison Hawley's demise.

Perhaps if Gary would have known he'd only have been even more intrigued, although perhaps he would have thought twice about applying for the job. Perhaps not as work, which didn't require hard labor for decent pay was hard to come by for a man in his position. Having no real work references or experience at that point made it very difficult for Gary to even land himself an interview.

Beggars can't be choosers.

A large sign which read: "CLOSED" hung on the front door when he walked up to the large gothic structure. Gary was told to simply head in and ignore the sign by the Mayor after his successful interview at city hall. City hall, what a joke. Gary had found it funny that the town was small enough that they had the Mayor conducting the interviews. He was the only staff member for the entire decrepit building beyond the janitor, who only came in at night because he held another job two towns over during

WESTING

his days. Times were hard in Westing for those who stayed or got stuck living their lives out within it's grasp. There had been three people waiting in the hallway to interview for the position when he arrived and two more had showed up after he left.

Gary guessed that jobs were hard to come by in a town as small and rural as Westing. The Mayor was rather blunt in his assessment of the task he would face, he'd be working for a miserable old stickler of a woman overnights and she wouldn't let it be easy. Luckily his new boss had gotten her fill of overnights as the clerk and Gary would only see her in passing at the begging and end of his shifts, the Mayor explained between pulls on his dwindling cigarette. Gary could have sworn he'd walked in on the man pouring whiskey into his coffee.

As Gary left the interview job in hand, he passed by

the group of downtrodden men all hoping to land the position he just had. Gary had felt more than a little guilty. These men were all just like him, down on their luck and hoping against hope for a fresh start. Two of the men were talking in hushed whispers while he walked out the door, he only caught a short portion of their exchange but indeed it peeked his interest.

"I hear Bartlett and Murray both quit the night it happened. I heard the sheriff didn't like their stories, said he thought they sounded like they weren't telling him everything. Maybe they had something to do with it?" The one man suggested to the other. "Maybe, I know Murray ain't been acting right but could you blame him? They watched her burn." The other fired back.

As intriguing as the conversation was Gary left

WESTING

without inquiring of the men about it as he was too happy at having secured the job. As soon as he got into his car he cried out of joy, making sure no one saw him of course so as to not rub it into anyone's face who might come out and see. On the drive home to his rat trap apartment he'd soon to be moving out of, Gary'd blasted the radio and sang along to all the songs he knew the lyrics to; like them or not. He was quite pleased with himself, quite pleased.

Gary Wettle was also quite pleased with the new apartment he'd landed in Westing. The rent was cheap and the apartment was large and isolated, which Gary loved. His landlord Mrs. Sullivan spent the majority of her time glued to her television drunk and out of his hair. The space was even furnished, bed, stove, refrigerator, luxurious for Gary at that point in his life. The drive from it to his new job at the library even went past a fantastic donut shop named Sally's and wasn't too far away. Sure the town was mostly filled with empty houses adorned with "For Sale", "For Rent" or "This building condemned" signs; but it was quiet and people kept to themselves. A quality of character most were a bit light on where Gary was from.

Gary pulled into the library's parking lot on that first night, the cement cracking and overgrown in spots. So overgrown in fact he didn't notice the sheriff's car until he was all the way parked. Sheriff Jeremiah Trahorn got out of his cruiser and sauntered up to Gary's car before he even had a chance to pull up the parking break. The sheriff sternly peered in through his passenger window, obviously looking over the interior of the vehicle as well as his person. Gary got out and greeted him, giving him his name and extending his hand.

The sheriff briskly shook Gary's hand after giving

him another look over and was polite but direct. He asked him his business and where he was from. Gary said he was the new custodian at the library. The sheriff chuckled, mentioning that a few people in town weren't happy about that, then welcomed him to Westing with a sarcastic smile. Gary thanked him and headed into the library, looking back over his shoulder to find the sheriff hadn't left the side of his vehicle or taken his eyes off of him.

It was a hard up town with less than fifty permanent residents; Gary was sure his hiring as an out-of-towner had rubbed more than a few folks the wrong way. He hoped the sheriff wasn't one of them. There wasn't a whole lot he could do if he was Gary reasoned.

Something else caught his eye on the way in, there was another car parked in the lot right in front of the building in a spot marked reserved. It was an old 1960 grey Buick station wagon that Gary assumed belonged to the dreaded librarian the Mayor had warned him about. The car had brand new tires, it's hood and chrome freshly buffed and shining in the dwindling daylight. "Looks like someone got a raise." He thought to himself.

When Gary first walked through the old library's large wooden arched doors he noticed the craftsmanship they contained. Intricate and ornate carvings adorned their faces. The whole building's construction, although very old, was indeed impressive. The wood carving was both detailed and well executed, although one could still tell it wasn't done by any master woodworker. In a way that was all the more striking to Gary as whoever had done the work certainly devoted themselves to it. There were portions that were obviously renovated more recently, and of course shoddily but the majority of the building was constructed remarkably well; even

WESTING

if it was archaic.

Gary's assessment of the property temporarily halted when he spotted Mrs. Culligan standing in the middle of the empty room, pouring over a large mess of books needing to be re-filed. She seemed to be struggling to categorize them. Her expression was flustered and unhappy to say the least. She looked exactly how he expected when the mayor described her. Mrs. Culligan was older and very thin, gaunt with deep lines in her aged skin; with wispy greying hair up in a tight bun atop her furrowed head.

Gary imagined that Mrs. Culligan very rarely wore any other expression than displeasure, she reminded him of his ex-wife in that regard. "A scowling miserable..." Gary tried to stop himself from thinking negative things, knowing no happiness would come of it.

"Save it for your books. In real life you can't blame others for reacting to the misery you caused. And it's no use to see the worst in anyone. Mrs. Culligan most likely is going to be difficult, but that doesn't mean you can't just ignore her negativity. Or simply endure it. You can deal with a difficult boss and live in a nice big apartment where your kids can come over and stay without sleeping in the same room. It's not a big deal. Stop worrying about things that haven't even happened yet." Gary reprimanded himself right before Mrs. Culligan noticed him with her piercing blue eyes.

"You must be my night assistant." She quipped in a rushed, condescending tone. "Come help me get these put away and then I'll show you your tasks for the evening." Before he could muster more than a nod, brushing a stray grey hair, which had escaped her bun from her brow to have a better look at him, she followed with another patronizing question. "You are familiar with the Dewey decimal system are you not? On your resume it said that you were and I do hope that wasn't a falsehood Mr. Wettle." Her tone was stern and off-putting but Gary managed a smile. It'd been quite some time since anyone had addressed him as Mr. Wettle, the last time he remembered was high school which indeed seemed a rather long time ago to Gary at that moment in his life.

"Yes of course, I've spent quite a lot of time in libraries, I'm a writer or at least I fancy myself one." He replied calmly with as much cheer as he could muster. "Good, because we have inherited a great deal of work and I can't be holding anyone's hand in getting it done." With that Mrs. Culligan shoved a pile of books into his arms, telling him everything he needed to know about her and how she intended to have things between them. He kept smiling, what else he could do about it he didn't rightly know. She informed him that she would observe him to make sure he was as capable as he'd claimed and did so for a few minutes until Gary proved himself.

After Mrs. Culligan left him to go sit in the comfort of her office with the door shut, Gary spent the next several hours sorting and filing the mass of returned books into their proper places amongst the rows. There were two very large floors filled with them. He found himself elated at the task, as it revealed to him the true enormity of the space. When he'd stopped to have a closer look at the library on his way back from landing the job it'd been closed and he'd only been able to peek into Mrs. Culligan's front office window and hadn't glimpsed the gigantic nature of the library inside. He'd guessed it to be much smaller and far less grand but was still exuberant at the prospect of overseeing so many wonderful volumes. Now Gary was almost as happy as he had been as a boy unwrapping presents on Christmas.

Gary'd always loved libraries, even as a child. His family never had much money, especially after his mother left; so that meant Gary's father would take him to their local library a lot. Books were always so mysterious and wonderful to Gary and as a child he often dreamed of having his own personal library, one filled to bursting with rare and exotic books. He'd owned a decent collection of volumes at one time when he'd been married but currently his collection wasn't anything more than a small stack of paperbacks laying atop his nightstand next to his alarm clock.

Gary promised himself that he'd work hard and get himself a lovely little private library in a giant home one day. At least he could dream and if he dreamt well enough he'd be able to escape to the place where it was real and that in itself was also beautiful.

Gary was practically salivating at the amount of older volumes Westing's library contained, some from as early as the 1700's. "A lot of these belong in a museum." Gary thought to himself but knew the township wouldn't let them go without some form of compensation or even entertain the notion. A town like Westing had scant resources as it was and he was sure they would be trying to squeeze every penny they could from what little they had. Regardless, the library was all and more than Gary had hoped it would be; a proper wealth of information and inspiration for his works. A quiet safe haven from his failed life.

"Stop referring to your life as failed. Your life isn't a

WESTING

failure and you're making the most of it." Gary wouldn't let himself think negatively or become morose about his past, something that he struggled with often. "One of the primary things that keeps people from achieving their goals is dwelling on their failures and letting them instill fear where there should be hope." Gary recited his mantras and tried to calm himself. Self correcting was one of the common themes, bad behaviors had to be replaced with more productive habits.

"One step at a time down the path is the only way." Gary knew he sounded like a nut job, one of those crazy people you meet who always has a smile on their face no matter what. The honest truth, undeniably; was that Gary had been terrified of where his life was headed if he didn't turn things around. Sure, he was enjoying his new found stability and sobriety; but most of all he wasn't scared for his life or sanity anymore. He'd been close to losing both and he knew it.

After finishing up the last of the books to be filed, Gary returned to the front office to find Mrs. Culligan routing through her desk's cabinets with a look of concern. He interrupted her unknowingly when he entered and she jumped slightly. "Goodness! You might have knocked!" She gasped then calmed herself. "I'm sorry, I've finished shelving the returns and the door was unlocked mam." Gary politely responded.

"All the same, knock next time." She replied coldly, then looked up at the clock. "At least you made short work of it, now I can go over the rest of your duties before I leave for the evening. Follow me." Mrs. Culligan quickly slipped some old papers off of her desk and into a drawer faster than Gary could make out anything on them but he did notice how nervously she'd hidden them from his sight and how startled she'd been.

WESTING

Mrs. Culligan promptly led Gary from the office, making sure to lock the door behind them. She was obviously put off by what he'd interrupted and seen but why Gary didn't know, so he brushed the feeling aside. They made their way through the ground floor of the building towards the back, then into a descending stairwell, which Mrs. Culligan had to unlock.

"Because there weren't any visitors today as we are closed for the week, you won't have to check to make sure everyone has left the premises tonight. Once we reopen you will have to do so every night before starting your custodial duties. I cannot stress enough to you how important it is that no one be on these premises after closing time, that includes guests or visitors of any type Mr. Wettle." She gave Gary a look that he knew all too well, the look of your job depends on this. He nodded and assured her no visitors would be found on his watch, her expression seemed less than convinced.

"The basement and third floor are solely used for storage and as I'm sure you've noticed the two floors between are active. As such unless instructed I want you to be allocating your time to them first and foremost. Now then, let's get started." Mrs. Culligan opened the door to the basement and waved that Gary should follow. He got a good look at her left ring finger, which was surprisingly not barren.

"Mind your step." She muttered as they descended without a hint of sarcasm, Gary thought immediately that she only cared that he not fall on top of her. He also noted that there was a third floor, something he hadn't noticed while he was putting away the returns. Getting returns to the second story was accomplished with the aid of a dumb waiter located just next to the front desk.

Just beside the contraption was the stairwell leading to the second floor, otherwise the task would be back breaking labor; something Gary was more than happy to avoid. It was obvious that the dumb waiter was added in a renovation, a mechanical beast running on gears amidst the time worn facade. Even it was itself a relic with age, although it certainly was in good repair; a common theme within the old building. The last improvements to the library hadn't been made anytime recently but the majority of what Gary had seen of the place was well maintained.

The stairs to the basement on the other hand looked to be in fairly bad shape, probably having never been replaced and certainly neglected. The rickety stairwell lead into a large basement sub level which also was filled with volumes and volumes of very old books, some even older than the ones Gary had spotted doing his returns. It was astonishing to him how thick the smell of heavy mold was in the air down in the library's cellar. The dim bare bulbs hanging were hardly light enough to see properly but Gary could discern that the mass of volumes was made up of a considerable number of unsalvageable books. The thrill of what the books might contain awoke a boyish spark of joy in his heart.

"This will be your task after you've finished cleaning the lavatories, sweeping and mopping the floors and of course re-shelving all the returns for the evening. I need the entirety of these volumes cataloged and the sorted. All of the books which are too far gone you'll pile over there by the outside doors to be disposed of in the dumpster. The rest can be cataloged and put back upstairs. I only want you down here for two hours every evening from closing until 10pm. After that you're to head back upstairs to the front desk to stand watch until I arrive at 6am. Sleeping is a fireable offense Mr. Wettle, I hope I've made myself clear." The old woman scowled without a hint of sarcasm.

"Perfectly." Gary replied, again forcing a smile. With that they headed back upstairs, although he felt pained to do so leaving such an unexplored treasure trove of old books alone in the dark to mold. Even if Gary had felt more unsettled in the underground space than the floor above, he had also felt more alive. The excitement of what volumes he might discover making his heart race.

Once Mrs. Culligan had shown him every item and cleaner in the broom closet and given him a lecture on the state of cleanliness she expected she gave Gary a set of keys, one for the front door, another for the basement and broom closet. She made quite clear he wasn't to be given a key to her office and again sternly warned him that venturing into that space would be cause for his termination. She would leave her wastebasket outside the door for him when it needed to be emptied.

"That's not a problem at all mam, I understand completely." He assured her, trying his best to endure her thinly veiled insults with a grin. Gary didn't like her one bit but he tried to be as polite as possible and smile in her presence. He wondered as she was leaving what kind of person would ever marry such an intolerable stickler, then found solace in the fact that it wasn't him.

Gary immediately checked his negativity, reminding himself that he had turned more than one woman's heart to stone and that he needed to focus on better things and be less judgmental and bitter. Better things like the piles of old books he'd just seen down

WESTING

in the basement.

"Focus on the good things Gary, just look at the bright side and do the work. Maybe she's just jaded about life because it's been hard for her? You know all too well about life being hard. Just don't let her get you down, it's just that woman's way of trying to pull you into her own sorrow. Sorrow's a lonesome lover, always looking for someone new." Gary reminded himself, trying to change his own intuitive responses from negative to positive wasn't easy but Gary Wettle genuinely was trying his best.

Sweeping and mopping didn't take up too much time and before long Gary was descending the stairs down into the basement again, his excitement boiling over. The lights flickered on in the dingy room and Gary made his way over to the mounds of books stacked neatest, deciding to rummage through the front of the pile. Wherein the stacks were orderly there, the books further in the back were heaped upon each other in a massively discordant fashion.

The front-most piles certainly were stacked with much greater care, even seemingly sorted to a certain extent. Gary quickly skimmed through all the spines for legible titles, trying his best to recognize any he may have read or any who's author may have been familiar. Much to his amazement he didn't.

After a cursory glance Gary was impressed by the collections size and variety. He was almost feeling overjoyed when he noticed another pile of volumes hidden away in the basement. In the corner by the stairwell leading back upstairs was a pile that looked to have been damaged in a fire, most were newer editions but all looked too fargone to keep. Gary decided to ignore them in loo of the other older volumes in better condition laid out in the piles in front of him.

He picked up the first book his hand happened upon, it's author unnamed with no title given. The book was written in Latin, of that much Gary was sure but beyond that he had no idea of it's context and quickly put it down on an empty desk to be a reference point for starting; separating it and moving on to the next volume.

The second book he picked up was in old English with an author who's name Gary couldn't recognize because it's inking had been blotted over, seemingly intentionally obscured but with a legible title; "The great riots of Westing". The book detailed an assortment of accounts of different residents of Westing, each attesting to the gruesome rioting, which occurred over a hidden treasure. A treasure

Gary put the book down on the desk to be gone over later when he'd be alone and moved through the rest of the immediate pile as quickly as possible, not wanting to be thought lax on his first night of work. Gary figured he would bring the book upstairs to peruse further but spent no more time on it and returned to his task.

There weren't many other titles of interest, only old census records, land deeds, news papers and other mundane or Latin volumes regarding the town of Westing; the latter of which he could only distinguish by the repeated utterances of it's namesake. After sorting as many of them as best as possible in his allotted time Gary headed back upstairs taking "The great riots of Westing." with him to examine while he spent his remaining hours waiting alone at the front desk.

WESTING

When Gary got to the top of the stairs he locked the door behind him and walked out onto the library's first floor. Gary was panicked to find that the front door was standing wide open. The wind was steadily blowing outside and some of the papers had been whisked from Gary's desk, fluttering through the air like leaves. He could see his own breath in the now freezing room. "Did the wind blow it open?" He asked himself.

Gary was sure he'd locked it behind the old bag when she'd left and this was the last thing he needed on his first night on watch. Gary quickly made his way over to the front door and closed it, giving a fast glance around outside to see if anyone was there. Finding the parking lot empty, Gary locked the front door and turned back around to the darkened library; regrettably having turned off all the lights before he headed downstairs to the basement earlier.

Gary felt like he was being watched from the darkness.

He could swear he even heard someone breathing, a faint shallow draw.

Gary scanned the dark library with his flashlight as he stormed over and clicked on the lights.

Waiting for the fluorescents to flicker to life seemed like an eternity to Gary, even though it was only a matter of seconds.

At last they sprung on and Gary promptly paced the first floor, checking every corner.

WESTING

Nothing seemed out of place.

Nothing that is until he came back to the top of the stairs leading down into the basement, which he swore he'd just locked.

The door was standing open.

Gary froze for a moment, listening for any signs of life, then decided to shut the door; making sure to lock it and to try the lock. He reasoned he'd check the basement before the end of his shift, if someone had gone downstairs he'd greet them in the light of morning. Gary walked back to the front desk, looking over his shoulder the whole way.

Once he reached the old oak desk Gary sat down, leaving the lights in the library on even though he knew Mrs. Culligan would scold him for it if she decided to stop by to check up on him. He didn't care, Gary wasn't easily shaken but both doors being open when he could have sworn he'd locked both had him on edge. He tried to distract himself, opening the book he'd found in the basement and skimming back to the last part he'd read.

Gary was about to start reading again when he noticed how filthy his hands had become from his work in the basement, so frustratedly he got up from his chair and took the short walk over to the lavatories. Gary washed his hands in the sink, looking back over the restrooms to make sure they were indeed clean. He knew that once Mrs. Culligan came in everything would be inspected first thing. Gary had a thought pop into his head as he

WESTING

scrubbed the filth off the side of the women's sink in a place he'd missed; Gary wondered what she was hiding in her desk drawer.

Gary pondered upon why the papers she'd so swiftly tucked away there in her office were of so great importance. Gary wasn't a thief, at least not of material things. Certainly in his youth he'd stolen the love of some women but Gary had never outright robbed anyone, even when he'd been completely destitute. Curiosity however was one of his dominant traits, he was after all a writer.

Gary finished up cleaning the sink and thoroughly washed his hands, deciding that whatever the unknown substance he'd just scrubbed from the porcelain didn't have any place on them. Gary wasn't a germaphobe by any standards but he did like to keep himself clean, so he took his time scrubbing them with soap and hot water until he was satisfied they no longer had any remnants of the scum.

When Gary returned to his desk everything seemed to be in order, the front door was still closed and all was quiet in the library. He moved to sit back down but had the thought to try Mrs. Culligan's office door, giving him pause. "See if someone got in there." Gary had the thought tempt him, trying to command him to go check and see.

"It's just a door. What do I care if it's locked?" Gary hesitated, trying to convince himself. The temptation remained. "That's how the devil brings you low. He gets you to do the wrong thing and then you'll do it again and probably worse next time. What's in that office is none of your business, it's a test. Do the right thing." Still curious, Gary wavered. There was

definitely something she was hiding but what?
"None of your business." Gary firmly told himself.
"None of your business if you want to do the right thing."

Gary decided against checking, thinking it'd be better if he didn't meddle with Mrs. Culligan's door. Instead Gary ran his finger over the aged parchment until; again he found his place in the old text. Yet again he had to stop before he started as he saw a similar large smudge of filth left over from the bathroom in almost exactly the same spot as before on his hand. Gary immediately shut the book, got back up and stormed into the bathroom; furious.

After scrubbing his hand clean Gary inspected both hands again, thoroughly. Affirming they were both spotless Gary took a paper towel and noticed the filth was on the dispenser. "On the god damn paper towel dispenser you animals!?!?" Fuming with rage Gary scrubbed the dispenser clean, going so far as to open it and clean out the inside as well. He then again washed his hands and cursed whatever filthy and perverse deviant would do such a horrible thing.

He was sure it'd been intentional and intended to inform Mrs. Culligan of it upon her arrival. Probably a delinquent or a transient Gary thought and had to catch himself from the same old negative thinking that he so often fell into. Nonetheless he thought it, the usual self deprecating lines of negativity. "A transient just like you were when you were living in your car? Go ahead and tattle to Mrs. Culligan about it. You're nobody. Worse, you're the person people hate. A looser. A bum." The thought echoed in the silence as Gary stood alone in the bathroom judging himself for all his own shortcomings and sins.

WESTING

"No matter how far you come or how high you fly your past will always try to lay you low." Gary thought. When Gary re-emerged from the bathroom he noticed that the old book he'd brought up from the basement was closed on the desk, he was sure he'd left it opened but couldn't be one hundred percent about it; especially in his current state. He wiped the tears from his eyes and was going to try and cheer himself up with a mantra when Gary felt the hairs stand up on the back of his neck.

Gary had heard something that he shouldn't have. The sound of a woman very faintly crying. It came from the second floor above him. Faintly but clearly. Ghastly and cackling, a tormented wailing unlike any Gary had ever heard before. The crash of lightning striking timber very nearby exploded just outside, less than a stone throw away from the library. The entire building lit up in a flash and the sobbing abruptly stopped.

He'd heard it nonetheless. Distinctly. Gary was sure of it, although he didn't want to believe it. He cautiously walked towards the stairwell leading to the second floor. Gary was about to go check on whatever had made the eerie sound, against his better judgment; when he heard the front door unlock and Mrs. Culligan burst inside.

"Why on earth are all of these lights on Mr. Wettle!?!" She demanded curtly. "I thought I heard a noise, maybe an animal; so I was just going to check upstairs. Figured it'd be better to not be looking for it in the dark." His answer and fake sincerity seemed to assuage her temper and the old woman's face took on a less enraged expression.

"Well at least you're not asleep behind the desk like I

expected. Strange weather we're having, supposed to storm on and off all week. Let's go see if there is indeed a vermin of some sort upstairs, you lead the way Mr. Wettle." Gary'd lied about it being an animal he'd heard and after his initial relaxation at having fooled Mrs. "I can't wait to fire anyone, lives forever in eternal misery." Culligan his fear returned. What indeed was on the second floor if not a vermin he dared not imagine?

Gary lead the way up the stairs, Mrs. Culligan following close behind him; closely enough that he could smell her bad perfume. "God the old bag really heaped it on." Gary thought as they ascended the stairwell. He hoped against hope she didn't fancy him romantically, though Gary was pretty sure she didn't fancy anyone in anyway; one never knows what carnal desires are harbored in the hearts of anyone.

Though it didn't seem to Gary that Mrs. Culligan was secretly lusting after him, a stern grimace never leaving her tightly pressed lips each time he glanced back to her on the stairs. There was something else he smelled underneath the odor of too much cheap department store fragrance, something fowl. Thankfully they stepped out of the closed in stairwell onto the second floor before he had to endure the odor any further and Gary was forced to pinpoint it's source.

Gary wondered what Mr. Culligan must think of his wife's work schedule, coming in at such an hour. He wondered a lot about Mr. Culligan. "Stop it Gary, you've got no room to make fun of anyone. Besides that you need to focus, suppose someone is in the library right now; this could cost you your job." Gary let none of his internal anxiety show as he held the door open for her, noticing that Mrs. Culligan also had begun to look less than enthusiastic about their undertaking.

WESTING

The upper floor was quiet, save the constant hum of the fluorescent lights hanging above them as Gary and Mrs. Culligan made their way through the rows of books. After surveying the entire floor and finding nothing, Gary noticed a locked door that he reasoned could only lead to the third floor. He walked over to inspect it.

"Well Mr. Wettle it seems you're hearing things." Mrs. Culligan muttered with a satisfied contempt. "Maybe it came from up on the third floor Mam?" Gary replied timidly to which Mrs. Culligan gave pause, almost as though she were afraid of what was to be found hiding in the floor above them.

"It couldn't be anything but vermin up there, keep the door shut Mr. Wettle and I'll call an exterminator in the morning." Mrs. Culligan had no sooner uttered the words when she turned round', almost trotting back towards the stairwell to the first floor. Gary took a moment before joining her, he knew in his heart what he'd heard wasn't any rat, squirrel or bird. It'd been the sound of someone crying, he was sure of it.

"Come now Mr. Wettle, I want to inspect your work before I start my own." Gary knew she was scared, maybe he should be as well but the bad part of him, the curious part; it wanted to know what was up on the third floor. Instinctively he obeyed her command, though even as he was walking away Gary kept thinking what secrets this old place held. Surely they were more than a few rats in the attic. Or whatever Mrs. Culligan was hiding in the drawers of the desk in her office.

WESTING

When they got back downstairs Mrs. Culligan went over every nook and cranny of the bathrooms, leaving Gary very pleased with himself and his decision to scrub them even if it had been disgusting. He had decided he'd keep the mess to himself, for all he knew it could very well have been anyone and not just a vagrant. More and more he was suspicious that it'd been Mrs. Culligan herself, he didn't put anything past her when it came to making his job miserable. Plus she had inspected the paper towel dispenser and he'd found that a bit odd unless she'd already known it was dirty.

Gary also noticed that it seemed as if the usually intimidating Mrs. Culligan was stalling, trying to avoid leaving the bathrooms to head downstairs and see his piles. Indeed after they'd finished in the bathrooms Mrs. Culligan informed Gary she would look at his basement work in the morning and hurried away to her office, closing and locking the door behind her. Gary was astonished and relieved, because honestly speaking Gary was more than a little terrified about going back into the basement; even with her accompaniment. He knew it was irrational, it didn't matter.

Gary clicked the lights off, then walked back to the front desk. He saw that the book, "The great riots of Westing." strangely lay open waiting for him, although he was absolutely sure he'd shut it. Yet the archaic text sat parted, illuminated in spotlight by the desk lamp. He slouched down in the old leather chair which was still very comfortable and began reading about the town's seedy history, murder and the extraction of justice only a mob can met out. In the end the town's three founders had vanished, most thought it was a sign of progress. Gary could only imagine what fate they'd met. Did they escape with the treasure, or was theirs a more sinister end?

WESTING

Usually when a mob is involved the later is true.

CHAPTER THREE: A NEW STORY.

Gary hadn't been so inspired in his life, at least not in a very long time. When he got home after his first night on the job Gary immediately sat down and wrote about the town of Westing. About a man named Herbert Skaghill living on the outskirts of Westing with his wife Loren, a couple whom had found a hidden room beneath their down trodden home while Herbert had been attempting to fix the plumbing. Herbert had seen the twinkle of gold coins deep within the crevice, he was sure of it but had made the mistake of telling Loren.

Herbert Scaghill had once loved Loren very deeply but time and Herbert's father in-law Jim had changed that.

Herbert got nervous when Loren told him she was thinking of telling her mother Betty, he knew that she wouldn't be able to keep a secret from anyone, much less her own domineering husband; nor did he want to split it with her tyrannical father. So Herbert lured Loren into the basement under the auspices of letting her try to reach the treasure, complaining that he was too large to fit through the hole. All the while waiting under the stairs until she took the first step.

Herbert Scaghill pulled his wife's ankle with all his might, sending her toppling headfirst down the

WESTING

stairs. Her neck and the back of her skull broke, along with the glass of gin and soda she'd been celebrating her husband's newly found windfall with. Herbert quickly covered the hole up, hiding the treasure and then promptly called the police; of course being as distraught as he could muster. Herbert told them through fake tears that Loren had fallen down the basement stairs, that she wasn't moving and to please send an ambulance.

The ambulance had to travel over forty-five minutes from the next town over to reach the scene, leaving sheriff Jeremiah Trahorn the lone first responder.

When the sheriff arrived he found poor Loren Scaghill stiff at the bottom of the steps with a highball glass lying shattered beside her. The glass was freshly stained with Loren's lipstick and contained the last un-spilled remaining sips of her heavily poured cocktail. Jeremiah Trahorn didn't think twice about what had transpired. Hell, he took Herbert out for a beer after the medics had drug poor Loren back up the stairs and off to the funeral home.

One of the medics even slipped on his way up the stairs, making it an open and shut book for the sheriff; a man who knew Herbert his entire life. He hardly suspected Herbert capable of anything as inhuman as cold-blooded murder, nor that Herbert had found a hidden treasure underneath his floorboards. What sheriff Trahorn knew of Herbert Scaghill was that he was a harmless man without a penny to his name and a wife whom he'd loved more than anything in the entire world.

He'd given up everything for the woman after all, choosing to stay in Westing even after the mine

WESTING

closed down just so they could be closer to her aging parents. Herbert Scaghill was a kind and tolerant man as far as Jeremiah knew, a man who'd just lost his beloved wife. He felt awful for him.

Gary poured himself a small glass of water, trying hard to stay away from the taste of whiskey. Charred oak held an appeal that he had loved so much it nearly killed him. Gary knew if he ever touched that fire water again he'd most likely lose his life, if not everything worth anything in it. Still, the old vice reared its head. Whiskey was absolution from the burden of caring, furthermore Gary found it delicious.

He thought of his son and daughter Caleb and Sarah and put the idea of tasting another drop from his mind. After all, writing stories of such morbidity was in and of itself his supposed one and only remaining vice and even of that he wasn't entirely sure. The work took a toll on him of that there could be no doubt. Always imaging the worst scenarios is brutal on any person's psyche, especially putting oneself into the minds of murderers and madmen as Gary often did.

"You can't mess up this time, you won't get another chance." The thought haunted him and Gary knew all too well that it was true, this was it; there wouldn't be any more do-overs. If he messed things up this time he'd be done for good. Gary couldn't live on the streets again, his body was too old to keep running into the ground and besides that if he lost the chance to mend his relationships with his children he might as well dig his own grave.

The faces he'd seen in the darkness around his campfire also haunted him but Gary did his best not

WESTING

to think of that.

"Keep focusing on the good things in a positive way, you're doing the right things today and trying your best." He reassured himself. "The stories you're writing are just that, stories; not vulgarity or thinly disguised smut." Gary knew the allure of playing in the gutter but was no longer fond of its charms. At least he was aware of the consequences. The faces he'd seen still haunted him, hallucinating or not it had seemed very real.

Still, it was hard from time to time for Gary to cut himself off from his vices entirely. Especially in his work. Gary found he had a taste for most of the macabre, although it did bring him shame with the knowledge that he had used it to bring harm to himself and the world through that fascination. That didn't mean he couldn't move past that and go for his dreams.

Gary was convinced that one day it would all pay off and he'd be able to buy a nice big house for his children to come stay as long as they liked in. That he'd write one huge hit and sail off into the sunset. Maybe he'd write children's stories and dime store adventure novels for fun. Travel the world, even after buying a mansion in his hometown near his children and father. There was a gigantic Victorian bed and breakfast that stood right down the street from his old house. The home where his ex-wife and children still lived. Gary sometimes imagined it was his. "Not bad goals to have." he thought. "Not bad at all."

Gary sat back down at the typewriter and hammered out the rest of the set up for the wife killer Herbert Scaghill, who upon reentering his basement later that night very drunk; went to begin battering down the rest of the wall which stood between him and his spoils. It just so happened that the sheriff came back to Herbert's house, having left his hat on the dining room table earlier. Hearing Herbert banging around down in the basement making one hell of a racket, the sheriff decided to take it upon himself to go see that his friend was ok; he reasoned Herbert had just lost his wife and checking up on him was only prudent.

As sheriff Jeremiah Trahorn soon discovered Herbert wasn't morning his late wife Loren, not one bit. He found old Herbert gazing intently into the hole that he'd made in his cellar wall, a hole from which the sheriff saw the beautiful glint of an abundance of gold. The glint made the sheriff reach for his second gun, the one he kept in his shoe for, "Just in case." moments. Just in case he needed a plant that was registered as stolen from the local gun shop, a place Jeremiah had the keys to. Open and shut case, "Herbert must have been suicidal after his wife's accidental death and broke into the gun shop. Tragic." Jeremiah was mentally already filling out the report as he crept up behind Herbert.

Herbert was so transfixed on his newly found fortune that he didn't notice the sheriff until it was too late, until the bullet was wedged in the back of the hidden chamber and the contents of his skull were all over the gold it contained. Jeremiah put the gun into Herbert's dead hand and quickly found a tarp to cover the gold with. He drug Herbert's corpse up the slippery steps and loaded him into his trunk, driving his body away to a secluded spot in the woods only the older locals even knew existed. Few, if anyone that had remained after the mine closed ever traveled that way anymore. The sheriff took Herbert's corpse to a place known as the honeymoon cut or lover's point, where young couples used to go "watch the sunset." When the town had been in better times. There weren't any young lovers in Westing anymore.

WESTING

Now sheriff Trahorn was dumping Herbert's corpse up in that once romantic thicket, which rather majestically overlooked the town proper. It had once been a truly beautiful view, back when there was money to be made in the mine and people raised huge families. Westing had been almost an idealistic place to live at one point, now most of Westing was boarded up and pretty much all the young and affluent people had moved away. The view of Westing from lover's point hadn't aged well, Jeremiah thought to himself as he battled the terrible terrain and thick swarms of mosquitoes which smelled Herbert's fresh corpse like Sunday dinner.

"At least no ones here." Jeremiah thought as he pulled Herbert's stiff corpse deep into the brush off the trail, making sure he went far enough away that the body wouldn't be easily spotted if indeed someone did happen to come around. Not that they would.

Sheriff Jeremiah Trahorn left Herbert Scaghill up there, tucked under a downed tree to rot covered by a thin layer of the fresh fall leaves. The sheriff was sure no one would miss him until it would all be circumstantial anyway. Besides, Jeremiah reckoned he'd be the one to investigate it. Herbert would just be one more lonely suicide in a town of lonely suicides. The town of Westing wasn't exactly known for much else beyond tragedy.

As a matter of fact Sheriff Trahorn had been so thoroughly numbed by the things he'd seen in Westing over his long career that he really didn't care very much about Herbert. If he were to be honest Jeremiah always had wanted to find a ticket out of the dying town of Westing. Sure he knew he

WESTING

should feel bad later but honestly Herbert hadn't felt any pain. The way Jeremiah reasoned it, the last moments of Herbert's life were overjoyed; he'd never seen it coming.

And although Jeremiah couldn't prove it, he wagered more than likely Herbert had killed Loren for the exact same reason he had done him in. There was a fortune buried in the recess behind the wall of Herbert Scaghill's basement, of that Jeremiah was sure. More gold coins than he'd ever imagined. Jeremiah thought it more than likely part of the original settlement's treasure that had never been recovered. It was a local legend, something they'd been told as kids. "Go look for the treasure!" His mother used to say it to him all the time when she wanted Jeremiah out of her hair.

The sheriff parked his car right in front of Herbert's

house, no one would question why of course Jeremiah smiled to himself. Herbert lived on a private road tucked away in the backwoods; the only folk who came around those parts were both dead now. The sheriff thought he had everything figured out nicely, even down to how he would pretend to find the old coins. He'd been meaning to fix up his house for some time, it stood to reason that if Herbert had found a treasure trove under his foundation than who would question him if he used the same story? If indeed he told anyone about them at all.

Gary had to stop typing for the day; he needed to sleep so he could stay awake for his shift that evening. He put the book he'd taken from his new job away, stowed his freshly typed pages in his nightstand and stretched out on his small bed. Sure it was a bed that was both stiff on his back and too short so his feet hung off, but Gary tried to look on the bright side of it. "It's ok, it's better than my car's backseat or a friend's couch or the street. Leave all the negative crap in your books." He reminded himself, smiling at the thought of his newest work. For the first time in a long time Gary knew what he was working on wasn't just good enough, it was actually good.

Gary went to bed and set his alarm, pulling the curtains as tightly as possible to avoid the sun from peeking through. He turned on the oscillating fan by his bedside and pulled the covers up over his head, forcing himself to try and sleep in spite of the fact that it was just before noon. Gary smiled at the idea, going to bed at this time was exactly what he'd always wanted to do as a writer. Getting to be awake late nights and working on putting together his stories was something he'd been trying to do his entire life. His best ideas often came in the middle of the night, perhaps because he was robbing himself of his own dreams. No matter what Gary was happier than he'd been in a long time, he cried a little to himself. Happy tears. The tears of a man who had been on the brink for too long and was just again finding signs of joy awakening within himself.

Gary's sleep wasn't as restful as he'd hoped, nor were his dreams beautiful, joyous or relaxing. Within his dreams Gary saw Murray Sax, the man who used to hold his position at the library as the overnight watchman. He was presently breaking into an abandoned mine shaft to mine out coal for money and to heat his home over the upcoming winter.

Murray would need to try and make enough of everything and save every penny to make it through till spring when he could potentially relocate. He pushed his largest wheelbarrow up the hill that lay just beyond the edge of his property, his truck parked tucked away in the thicket not far off. He planned on making several runs to fill the truck bed.

WESTING

It wasn't the first time in his life Murray had to resort to this, after the mine shut down he'd done it quite frequently up until he'd landed his recently former job at the library.

Not that he would ever go back to that place, even if it meant mining coal alone at night in October. Everything was open to Gary about Murray, his mind's workings merging with his own. He knew what Murray was doing was extremely dangerous; he'd almost gotten lost once before in the shaft going in alone. Times were bad and he'd rather face the mine than what he'd seen in the library. Gary tried hard to dig through Murray's memories and see what that was but it was in a part of Murry's mind that was sealed off, more than likely out of fear Gary reasoned.

Gary floated up the hill and watched as

Murray expertly ripped the boards off the entrance with a hammer, obviously having performed the operation many times. Murray set the boards off to the side of the entrance and walked into the darkness of the mineshaft a short ways before turning on his headlamp. Gary followed him into the darkness when suddenly he was pulled out of the tunnel and thrown through the forest at an impossible speed, soaring over treetops to Herbert and Loren Scaghill's dilapidated old house.

The Scaghill's recently vacant house was darkened save a light on in the basement; the sheriff's car was still parked out front. Loren had decorated the lawn with a village of garden gnomes and the little statues peered at Gary from under the dead October grass. Their eyes were alive, eerily staring at him. It was daytime out, but the secluded home and surrounding forest seemed excessively dark in the day's all encompassing gloom.

WESTING

An overwhelming sense of malice and threat hung in the cool fall air. Gary could instinctively feel that there was immense danger inside of Herbert's house. What was worse than how he felt was the fact that he wasn't able to stay outside, even though he desperately struggled to.

Gary wanted to leave, he wanted to wake up.

It was useless for him to resist, because no matter how hard he tried to leave Gary was being drawn to the front door. Pulled towards it by some invisible force. He knew something horrible was waiting for him inside the house, something that in spite of his overactive curiosity; he did not want to see.

Something that wanted to see him.

Gary floated up the driveway and over the cobblestone path to the old wooden door. It was closed, locked. There was a low growling coming from far away, deep within the home.

Gary couldn't resist it, he had to open the door; whatever was in Herbert's basement wanted to see him. It knew Gary was there and he could feel it's eyes on him, it didn't matter if there were walls and floors between them; it could see. It was controlling him too. Very slowly breaking his will and forcing Gary to come up to the door.

Gary reached out his hand to turn the knob.

WESTING

The sounds of cruel grunts echoed from inside closer and closer. Something was climbing the basement stairs, something heavy. In the window's glass Gary could see that the lawn gnomes had all turned to watch him, the windowpanes rattled harder and harder as the thundering footsteps approached.

The door swung open but before Gary could see what was waiting on the other side he awoke to the sounds of his cheap bedside alarm clock ringing in his ear.

Beep! Beep! Beep!

Gary got up and ready quickly, showering less than his usually long soak; which was now a fixture of his days since coming off of the street into a place of his own. The hot water reminded him of how lucky he was to have it. However on this day Gary wanted something more than comfort, he wanted to write. He made short order of eating his waking meal of leftover beans and sausage and got right to pouring out the words to his story onto the page. A story made all the easier to imagine because of his recent vivid dreams.

Gary sat down and wrote as fast as his fingers could strike the keys about what happened when the sheriff went back to Herbert's home and what he found in the basement. Rather, what he didn't find. There was no treasure, no gold coins under the tarp as the sheriff had seen earlier. Only blood and pieces of Herbert's skull and brain matter.

Jeremiah ransacked the entire home, knowing someone must have come by while he was dumping Herbert's body. Someone who had stolen the treasure right out from under him. Someone must have seen him kill Herbert Scaghill.

But who?

The sheriff kept thinking over and over of all the possible suspects. No one fit the bill. Unless Herbert didn't know someone was watching him when he had initially found the treasure, someone must have been watching the entire time. "Maybe his wife had known and told someone? Maybe that old man who was his wife's father came by and saw me after they heard the news. If not them who could it be?" He didn't know. That meant big trouble for sheriff Jeremiah Trahorn. That meant someone knew he was a murderer.

The first thing the sheriff did was drive immediately

over to the family of Loren Skaghill. When he arrived he found Betty and Jim Linkler in mourning over the loss of their only daughter, if it was an act they had him convinced. Not once did the Sheriff detect a hint of fear or discomfort from either of them, only deep sorrow and loss. All the same, they'd have to be tested; too much was at stake.

After hours of savage beating and death threats the Sheriff all but concluded they indeed had known nothing. Getting rid of their bodies had been exceedingly less difficult as a stream passed right down the hill from their residence. The plot of deeply secluded land had several mountain streams, the lot of which flowed into caves at the properties base.

After watching the couples bodies disappear into the rapids, Sheriff Trahorn made his way back to the Scaghill residence hoping whoever had stolen the

WESTING

treasure had left a clue. Pulling up to the home the Sheriff noticed that it seemed like someone had arranged the lawn gnomes so that they were all watching him. He shook it off, rationalizing that Loren must have intended that effect and he'd just never noticed it. In fact had the Sheriff had more time to focus on the eeriness of it, he might not have gone back inside.

The door stood open, even though the Sheriff was absolutely sure he'd locked it behind himself. "Someone's still inside." Jeremiah thought to himself as he freed his gun from it's holster. Why the thief would return didn't make sense to the Sheriff and his mind riffled through the possible reasons. His first instinct was to head back down into the basement and upon his ascension into its depths he was awestruck, the treasure had returned; gleaming back at him from the hole in the wall.

ADAM AHLBRANDT

The exhilaration had his heart thundering in his chest as Sheriff Jeremiah Trahorn walked over to the darkened hole and gazed upon the magnificent stash of gold nested there. He let the coins slip through his fingers as he grabbed a handful, just to make sure they really were what they seemed to be. It was rather unbelievable and Jeremiah was already on edge when the sound of someone tapping on the basement window came from behind him.

Tap.

Tap.

Tap.

WESTING

The Sheriff spun round and charged towards where he swore the knocking had come from. No one was outside that Jeremiah could make out in the dwindling daylight, at least; not at first. A mist had begun to hang over the lawn and conspicuously; Jeremiah noticed how again every lawn gnome he spotted seemed to be turned to face him.

Looking out the basement window and seeing them staring blankly from all corners of the lawn, now at eye level was unsettling enough; when a group of figures not made of fired clay emerged from the mist then vanished in an instant. It was Loren Scaghill and her parents, their blank gazes boring through Jeremiah; chilling him to the bone.

"It's just not real. You're imagining it." Jeremiah told himself, his eyes never leaving the lawn as he continued to search for the phantoms he'd just seen.

ADAM AHLBRANDT

The gathering mist and fading light-making visibility almost a few yards at best. A light whistling of the wind rattled the basement window that sat loose in it's frame after years of neglect and after a long while Jeremiah had convinced himself that the knocking he had heard was just a product of it's rotten caulking.

Jeremiah gave up looking at the lawn any further and walked back over to the treasure. He still didn't have a rational explanation as to where the gold had vanished to or how it had miraculously returned. "You haven't slept a wink and a lot has happened, you're exhausted; seeing things." The Sheriff told himself calmly, not believing a word of it. In his heart he knew what he'd seen and that indeed the dead were outside in the twilight, hiding somewhere in the mist.

WESTING

Jeremiah packed up the gold, quickly piling it onto the tarp; his hands shaking with fear. All over his body Jeremiah Trahorn felt the cold stare of death, his skin poxed with goose bumps; his teeth chattering. As a boy he'd had nightmares about someone watching him. Someone he could never see but who he could always feel, watching. Jeremiah's mother had told him to pray but he'd had the dreams in spite of his pleas to an un-answering god.

Jeremiah Trahorn's worst dreams were about to come true. As he finished digging every last coin out of the dirt and piling them on the tarp he heard a sound, sharp and intentional. A hard rasping knock, struck three times against the basement window.

Bang!

Bang!!!

BANG!!!

The blows thunderously echoing in the eerie late afternoon silence. Jeremiah turned to see Herbert's dead face pressed against the windowpane, his hair full of dirt and leaves; his features expressionless save his eyes. Herbert's unblinking eyes followed Jeremiah as he dashed towards the stairs, conveying the suffering they intended to witness befall him.

Sheriff Jeremiah Trahorn rushed up out of the basement but in his haste his footing was lost on the steep stairs and Jeremiah went tumbling down into

WESTING

the basement in much-the-same way Loren Scaghill had, for although Herbert didn't physically touch Jeremiah as he did his wife; he did very much so cause the accident. Only the sheriff didn't die immediately from the fall, he only broke part of his spine.

As he lay dying Jeremiah could see the hole that Herbert had smashed in his foundation wall, someone was inside of it watching him die; someone lurking in the dark. Jeremiah was paralyzed from his injuries unable to do more than scream which he did until his voice went horse. In the silence thereafter Jeremiah heard the sounds of the basement window opening and Herbert crawling through.

Jeremiah's death mimicking the one he had bestowed upon Herbert Scaghill, only it wasn't treasure he was looking at in that dingy basement hole; it was the glint of two unblinking eyes staring from the darkness. The sounds of Herbert pulling his corpse across the filthy floor echoing in his ears louder than a gunshot.

Gary had to leave and quickly put away his typewriter onto the shelf, stowing the newly written pages into his bedside nightstand's top drawer. He felt great about having such quality within the work. "Maybe my old publisher would be kind enough to at the very least read it. I'm not writing filth anymore and Carl will see that." Gary thought with hope.

"If not I'll just self publish the book, try and get a few of the smaller local stores to carry it. After all a murder mystery always sells, people always want to find reasons other than the true nature of reality to be scared. They buy dreams of death and horror to distract themselves from their own boring realities."

WESTING

Gary did as well. Almost everyone he knew did too, in one way or another.

Escapism is what makes the world go round and the world wants blood.

It was however something Gary tried to do less and less, unless he was the one creating it at that point. Because spending time reading other people's bad dreams wasn't getting him any closer to achieving his own good ones. Gary tried to limit his indulgences to what he considered research or what he watched with his children.

They loved horror movies just as much as he did. All the old universal pictures were their favorites and the local theater near them played all those wonderful titles regularly during the matinees. They especially would have a great day together when an old western was played following the horror feature, usually a perfect way to get one's mind off the terror; cowboys and gunfights. Cherry coke and popcorn, lots of fried chicken afterwards; those were Gary's favorite moments.

That same theater was now playing The Texas Chainsaw Massacre to sold out crowds. A film Gary had decided not to see in spite of it's raging success, he just would rather not have to watch anything so brutal. Gary was aware of how hypocritical he was being, writing the story he currently was but Gary noticed how terribly it affected him to ingest truly violent and horrific works. Besides that Gary had enough nightmares of his own.

The faces.

WESTING

The eyes.

"Stop it. Don't think about it." Gary quickly made his way to the library, still arriving early as he knew Mrs. Culligan was someone who you either kept happy or you weren't employed by. He simply looked at it as a means to an end. It was an opportunity he had to take, a path to follow that seemed to hold promising returns. So he would endure it. "Make your dreams come true by working for them." He repeated the mantra.

"You've wasted your life." A voice in his head answered.

Gary tried to refocus his emotions, get them away

from looking only at the negative. Reading a lot of self help books he'd indeed seen the changes in his own life by following their advice. "Just keep looking at the good things and you'll be alright." Gary reassured himself as he climbed out from his car's front seat, his old standby where he had slept so many nights. He glanced around the parking lot for the sheriff's cruiser but found nothing. In a way Gary was a little let down, he'd wanted to get the officer's real name; as well as memorize his face better.

Gary's dream about the Sheriff had seemed so much more detailed than what he remembered of the man when they met in real life. Gary naturally was curious to compare reality with his dream version of the Sheriff. He let the disappointment go, Gary was sure to see him around sooner or later and more than likely; he'd be sorry when he did. Mrs. Culligan had explained the prior evening that the Sheriff used the parking lot as a way to catch unwanted guests coming into Westing before they made it into town.

WESTING

The library was the unofficial check point of Westing. It'd stood watch on the hill over the town, which lay down in the valley below since it's founding. Anyone who wanted to go into or come out of Westing had to use the main road situated just out front in of the library.

There was also an access road around the back of the building that lead directly to the highway but Gary and the general public were strictly forbidden from using it. Gary chuckled at way Mrs. Culligan had wagged her finger at him while denying him access to the road. "It's only for official government vehicles." She'd admonished him when he inquired about using it.

Westing was a little town in the middle of nowhere

with one way in and out, locked away from the rest of the world; surrounded by mountains and untamed forest on all sides. Looking at it from the vantage of the library steps you could see that at one time, not too many years gone past; it'd been an almost Norman Rockwell representation of the classic American small town.

"Maybe it's best days are behind it but it still has some of it's former magic. Even in ruin it's still got a sort of charm." Gary thought as he peered over the once thriving, now clinging to life settlement. It sure looked beautiful to him in the fading daylight, floating in a sea of the autumn painted forest. A forest who's colors still ranged from verdant, to warm yellows and golds; even bearing vibrant crimson hues and deep rusty earthen tones in the fading daylight.

Gary was grateful for everything in his life, the view,

his happiness; even the chilly fall breeze. "The world is still a beautiful place, you just have know where to look." Gary reminded himself as he admired the old town, his self-help really seemed to be working and Gary was more than a little proud of himself for the changes he'd been making. He headed in, putting his worries from the night before behind him. Gary resolved to enjoy what he could of the time he spent at that lovely, if not a bit frightening; mysterious old building. "Make the best of it. Always make the best of it."

Gary's second night started out a bit better than the first as they weren't due to open the library back to the public until the end of the week, so the workload was light. Gary had filed all the outstanding returns the day before and only two total new books were to be put back from that day. This meant he wouldn't have nearly as much work as on the previous evening. Gary quickly filed away the two returns and set about cleaning the premises, all the while Mrs.

Culligan stayed in her office with the door locked. He might have been wrong but it seemed like Mrs. Culligan was relieved to see him when he arrived.

In fact he thought she had looked a little bit nervous.

Scared even.

Gary noted it but paid it no mind and instead finished his janitorial work, then headed down into the basement to get back to sorting through the wonderful piles of old books. He was mostly over the scare he himself had gotten the night before, although when Gary unlocked the basement door the hairs were standing up on the back of his neck. A voice in his head spoke to him, the morbid one. It was just for a second and Gary had been able to

WESTING

shut it up by walking down into the darkness but it had been loud and clear. It told Gary that something was waiting for him in the dank basement, something was watching him; something dreadful. As a matter of fact he felt watched at all times in the building.

Gary did his best to shake it off. It was only a feeling and if he was being honest with himself he didn't know if he'd been having residual effects from his bad LSD trip. Gary had only seen one thing since that experience that had been frightening to him and seemed connected. It had however, been tangible and not anything that Gary could chalk up to hallucinations; a fact that made it all the more disturbing. Gary had again seen a small hand print on the outside of his car's window, smeared into the condensation; one morning a few days after his initial incident at the campsite.

"Anyone could have done it, a kid as a prank; anyone." Gary thought about how silly it was, here he was a grown man with two children worried about the LSD he'd taken. "Maybe you shouldn't have messed around with drugs you bought from a guy who smells like a dead dog and that's missing the majority of his own teeth." Gary chuckled as he flicked on the bare overhead bulbs and began sorting through the old volumes. The only thing in the basement with Gary was his lonesome and a mess of dusty old books. His paranoia had seemingly been for nothing.

Still, there was something unnerving about the space. The air was so musky with mildew and mold Gary had tied off his handkerchief around his face like the Lone Ranger, or a bank robber. He'd always loved a good heist story, even as a child imaging getting away with a fortune was one of his favorite daydreams. He mused to himself that perhaps he would find a rare edition hidden within the heap as he sifted through the stacks and that it would set him up for life.

Gary found that the majority of the older texts were in old English, with a few in Latin and while a portion of the pile was salvageable; a great deal were not. The basement floor was wet in places, looking like it had flooded more than once over the years, ruining the volumes that had sat in it's dingy cradle. Of course that left anything sitting about a foot or so from the floor, soaked and rotten beyond repair.

Gary first worked his way through everything he could see was still salvageable and written in old English, starting within the first pile. Neatly taking it and stacking it by the stairwell door on crates, to keep what was worth keeping safe. He tried his best to elevate all of the newly sorted good volumes off the floor, knowing a storm was expected in the coming days and not wanting to have to repeat his efforts. Gary then stacked the remaining texts that were in Latin on the rusting sheet metal desk, figuring he should head up for the evening as he'd almost used up the allotted two hours. He didn't want any trouble from the always-cheerful Mrs. Culligan, so being punctual was something he'd tried to adhere to; regarding everything with her involvement.

When Gary made his way upstairs he found much to his delight that Mrs. Culligan had already gone, leaving him alone for the evening. He double-checked that the basement and front doors were locked, tapping both three times to remind himself of that fact.

Tap.

WESTING

Tap.

Tap.

Gary was using a trick he'd learned from one of his many self-help books. It was supposed to aid him in remembering things by drawing attention to the action with a repetition of another action. He was hoping it'd get him in a routine of making sure to lock every door in the building behind himself, every time. Basically his entire job consisted of only that responsibility for the duration of his shift. That and keeping the lights off and himself awake were the majority of his duties every night, or so Gary ascertained from his one and a half nights employed.

What he did with the time in between when he was free was his to use as he pleased. A rather ideal situation for him to have, volumes of books to inspire him and time to jot his inspirations down. Unlike at other times in his life, Gary intended to use his time wisely. His new book had already begun to take form; in fact the story had been organically flowing from his fingers without the need to pause to find the right words or punctuation. It just seemed to call to him in a way he couldn't ignore. Gary wanted more than anything to get back to his typewriter and keep pounding away but at least while he was in the library he could do the next best thing, research.

Gary set about finding a book regarding Latin to English translation, seeing that it may come of some immediate use to him; as a good portion of the books he assumed contained Westing's sorted history were in that language. Gary hadn't learned it as his parents weren't Catholic or even church going people, his father often telling him as a young boy that church was what you did every day; kindness and mercy didn't need any home outside of your heart.

After consulting the filing cards he came up with a few titles that fit the bill, all located on the second floor just by the stairwell. He was in luck. Gary didn't want to admit it to himself but something about the third floor terrified him and he didn't want to go anywhere near it, even the door leading up to it. All he would have to do was make his way to the second floor right by the stairs and quickly retrieve the book. He'd be in and out, off the second floor and nowhere near the third floor entrance.

Gary could tell himself all he wanted that he was suffering from exhaustion, having flashbacks or residual hallucinations; he could only half accept that as an explanation for everything that'd been going on in the old building. The sounds of crying hadn't just been his imagination, or any remnant of a bad hallucination. Gary wasn't convinced that any vermin could sound so human or that his mind had just been playing tricks on him. Still, what Gary did know of psychotropic drugs lead him to keep in the back of his mind that his perception couldn't now always be trusted, no matter how real anything he'd heard or seen may have seemed.

Gary kept replaying in his mind how Mrs. Culligan had scurried away from the third floor when he'd suggested they check it. Her fear was plain as day and he remembered it had unnerved him to his core. It wasn't often that Gary saw someone afraid to that degree, he'd seen the tips of her fingers trembling as she scampered away towards the stairs.

"Be brave Gary. Cowards don't write great stories

WESTING

and you're not a coward. Keep your head together." The voice from the night prior was what kept Gary on edge, the one softly crying from the floor above him. He kept returning to it, the raspy voice's weeping had a strange timbre. The tone and pitch had sounded hollowed out, like the throat and lungs of it's origin were charred. It didn't make Gary a coward to fear it, it made him a reasonable man.

Still, he wanted to know what mysteries the library held about the town of Westing within it.

That meant going to the second floor, alone.

"Come on, you're wasting time. You've got to get to work on your story and this is part of it. You know exactly where it is and it won't take more than a few seconds." Gary pushed his fear aside and quickly made his way up the steps, retreating back down them immediately after retrieving the volume of his concern; not even bothering to look in the direction of the door to the third floor.

He never stopped feeling watched the entire time.

Once back to his desk Gary realized his error, not having brought any volumes needing translation up from the basement. Now it was dark and he was alone, not that it should have mattered; but it did. He again thought about chickening out and waiting until the following day to start the translations. Mrs. Culligan would again have him work on the piles downstairs but it was so early in the evening, Gary knew that he had a long night ahead either way. He knew he needed to use the time wisely, so again he mustered his resolve.

WESTING

Gary forced himself to get up, take his flashlight and head to the back of the building.

The lights being off didn't help Gary from dreaming up morbid scenarios in his head. "Stop it, you're not writing." He told himself firmly, trying to keep his focus positive as he walked towards the basement stairwell. "It's just an old building, you can go anywhere in it you like."

Gary stood at the door and confidently reached into his pocket to produce the key, however his hand found nothing but lint. He'd left his keys sitting on the top of the desk back at the front of the building. "Just like always Gary. Always the idiot." He admonished himself in his mind before stopping himself and trying to redirect his thoughts.

"Just go back and get the keys, its no big deal. Stop being so hard on yourself, you don't have to be in a rush to do anything tonight. Just a short walk, that's all it is. You're not an idiot, yes you've made some stupid choices in your life but you know better now and you're trying. That's all that matters. Everyone makes mistakes, has regrets and shame. You're doing the right things right now, relax."

Gary got the keys off the top of the desk and walked all the way back to the basement stairs in no time at all. This trip his fear had diminished considerably as Gary chuckled at having been so hard on himself over such a trivial thing. There wasn't anything to be angry about, he was just overly emotional and needed to get ahold of his anger. It certainly hadn't served him well in his life. There wasn't anything to fear or be upset over; everything was about focusing on the task at hand and making the most of it. Gary

WESTING

unlocked the door with ease, walking down the darkened stairs into the basement; flicking the old bare bulbs back to life once he reached the cellar floor.

Gary relaxed enough to take his time picking out what Latin volumes seemed of the most interest to him, admiring the finer bindings and parchment some had and the crude age of others. Gary settled on three books to try and translate for the evening, two of which had superb craftsmanship and one which seemed to have been a diary or personal account.

"Write your ticket." Gary told himself as he flicked off the lights and walked back up the stairs, leaving the basement dark. He then headed for a hot cup of coffee and an attempt to translate Latin. He felt up to the task and made sure to lock the basement door behind him, then tapped the key on the door three times.

Tap.

Tap.

Tap.

"Self help really works. Just help yourself see the best outcomes for your own life then logically work towards them." Gary chuckled as he recalled the infomercial he'd ordered his first book from and all of its cheesy catch phrases but also knew that what the message was at its core was indeed true. "No one is going to help you in this world if you don't help yourself." Is what his father had told him when he'd asked for a place to stay after the divorce, shutting the door in his face. Gary had been angry with him for it at first but deep down he always understood his motives.

He had been a burden and a user.

Gary could admit that now, it took a lot but he had finally let go of his ego on the matter. Life isn't for the weak and more importantly it doesn't favor those who don't do the right things or enjoy what happiness it provides. "Take as much pleasure from your days as possible but not at anyone's expense." Was one of Gary's favorite self-help mantras. He knew all too well that good times are gone too quickly and if you hurt people bad times weren't far off.

ADAM AHLBRANDT

Everything has a way of coming back to you.

The hot coffee brewing got Gary excited to be alive, "If only it had a little nip of whiskey in it." He thought and quickly corrected himself. "I like it both ways. I'm grateful to not be drunk, down and out on the street. Coffee with plenty of fresh cream and sugar is fine enough." Indeed the coffee was delicious, it along with the sugar were leftover from the previous employees in the drawer of his desk. He was more than grateful for them.

The cream Gary had brought himself from Sally's in his small cooler, which doubled as a lunch box, the staff had been short to the point of rudeness; he'd brushed it off. The cooler was another relic from his life on the road where owning a refrigerator was an impossibility. He'd kept hotdogs and eggs on ice in it during the summertime to cook on his lone cast iron skillet over his campfires. That was until he stopped making them.

His writing during those dark times had been low of that Gary had no doubt. He'd stooped to taking vulgarity into his craft and had lost his publisher. Too many whiskey filled nights under the forest darkness. Too many garden hose showers stolen on stranger's lawns at midnight or in rest stops being judged by everyone who walked in. He'd kept the bottles in the cooler as well, hidden under all of the ice he'd steal from the local motel vending machine daily. Bottles and bottles of whiskey to keep him company in the dark around his lonesome fires, or later in the back seat of his car curled up just to fit. Whiskey and a pad of paper with a pen as his weapon against himself and the world.

"Stop dwelling on the past, it's a dead end." Another of his favorite mantras, Gary knew all too well that was the truth. "It's hard to let go and move forward but that's the only real way to try to do things better. Get back to work. If you dream you can make something worth dreaming about." Gary also knew that was the truth and so he set himself to his dreams.

Gary began translating the first text, one of the two finer looking of the three; he was disappointed to discover it was nothing more than a medical compendium of an outdated time. He moved on to the next book only to find a similar result, this one a text on the studies of various known drugs and their organically occurring variants in nature. At least the coffee was good Gary thought, it's sweetness and cream ratio was just right for his palate. It was piping hot too, the perfect temperature on a cold October evening.

WESTING

Gary savored it.

The last book he brought up from the basement proved to be the most interesting. After translating only a few words Gary's suspicions were confirmed, the book was indeed a diary. The diary was extensive; spanning what seemed to be decades. From his translations Gary could surmise that the author was a monk who had lived in England and that the document began sometime in the year 1642.

The monk was a young man who had freshly taken his vows named brother Jonathan Hawley. There were the usual prayers to god and daily thoughts on life in the monastery, typical of any monk; written in a fine hand in the beginning of the journal. Gary was ready to give up on it due in large part to it's exhaustively scrupulous detail of a mundane existence and endless prayers which seemingly had nothing to do with the town of Westing when he translated something that caught his attention. It was a line about war and men fleeing to the monk's monastery seeking aid for their wounds and sanctuary from the terrors of battle.

The war battered men were part of an uprising that sought to usurp the then king of England, Charles I. The monk detailed in the manuscript how the Catholic Church and any who appeared sympathetic to its traditions were hated in the eyes of the puritan revolutionaries. Puritans who lined the pews of the simple church Jonathan Hawley and his fellow brothers attended to. Supposedly, in the quest to enlighten all of their souls to god's great plan and of his mercy towards all of mankind. The king who's wife was of Catholic descent, held sympathetic views towards the Catholic Church and therefore fell out of favor with his own people and parliament. Because of this the entire nation had fallen into civil war.

When war broke out within their countryside Jonathan and his fellow brothers took mercy upon the wounded puritan soldiers, tending to their wounds; feeding them and offering them shelter. It was a gruesome time for brother Hawley who saw the horrors of war and consoled more than one dying man.

Jonathan Hawley however still held dear in secret to several of his Catholic upbringings and even though it would have spelled his execution, most likely at the hands of those same revolutionary soldiers who's lives he was saving; he practiced secretly writing his diary in their preferred holy language. Brother Hawley confessed in his journal to hating that they had refused to treat the Catholic wounded in the fighting, he said it felt sinful to turn them away.

Jonathan Hawley felt responsible for the deaths of all who'd perished outside their closed doors.

In these times Jonathan Hawley confessed to having pondered the nature of human evil and why god would allow it to exist. Why men were so driven to hate simply by the slight differences within their practices of worship. Why they could justify outright murder, torture and all other manners of sinful debauchery in the name of salvation. He'd seen brother turn against brother, committing countless atrocities in the name of the god they purported to serve. Brother Hawley had seen the outright slaughter and sadistic torment men meted out upon their fellow man in the name of having the proper religion.

WESTING

These were Jonathan's charges.

Men whom he'd given the Holy Communion.

It seemed to all mean nothing.

Gary skipped ahead in the diary as the monk spent a good deal of time pondering the great mysteries of his faith and although the weight of it was compelling, Gary grew tired of the repetitious pleas to god and questions of the esoteric. He finally found more historical passages and resumed further translation of the text.

The year in the monk's diary was now 1648 and the

nearest city to the monastery, Colchester was under siege. Loyalist forces of king Charles I. were surrounded by the puritan army and had taken the city's populace prisoner in an attempt to keep the puritans from attacking. Thinking foolishly that the threat of risking the lives of so many innocent members of their own faith would sway the hearts of the puritan army away from laying siege.

They were wrong.

Jonathan Hawley watched the city burn at the hands of the puritan onslaught, losing many of his own loved ones to the barbaric act. The siege lasted months, the townsfolk starved and the city turned to rubble. No one spoke of it in the brotherhood. They were told only to pray.

WESTING

Pray to god while the innocent starved and bled.

Pray while the city burned and the cries of the dying hung on the ashen winds.

Pray but not act.

A few children escaped the besiegement, fleeing to Jonathan's monastery with horrific tales of the conditions inside. Tales of cruelty from both sides, of despair and desperation, destruction and the struggle to survive. House pets had become meals within the ruins… So had the dead.

These children had to be hidden from the puritan forces by Jonathan and a few of his brothers who refused to let the orphans fall into the puritan army's hands, as they were at risk of being put to death if discovered. All residents had been deemed as traitors. The guise of holy deeds couldn't disguise the outright murder being committed in the name of god from any who chose to see it.

No longer finding the pious beauty in the puritan faith he had once held so dear, brother Jonathan Hawley decided to take counsel with his most trusted childhood friends; Levi and Abernathy. The men formed a plan to escape war torn England to the new world with a group of their families and friends, a land which brother Hawley had seen transformed from hope and prosperity in his youth to outright war and plague in his young adulthood. America held the promise of peace for them that England no longer could.

WESTING

Still, brother Jonathan Hawley held a troubled heart about absconding the land of his birth with stolen gold when the country was so desperately in a time of enormous strife. He decided to beseech the heads of his order that they might see a way to end the misery of the current war so blighting England. They surely could end the combat and try diplomacy instead, Jonathan rationalized that more bloodshed certainly wasn't what the church would want.

He was wrong.

The prolocutor, Jonathan's direct superior, only told him that men are given the choice between good and evil; that it was the contract that god had given them and only god himself could intercede in stopping the war. The prolocutor also told brother Hawley that sometimes you have to choose the lesser evil to do the most good and that was what the church was trying to do with the current conflict.

A conflict that Jonathan Hawley could plainly see was funded from the church's own coffers, who's puritanical front he now begrudgingly knew all too well was only a farce. Jonathan Hawley decided then that men could not be trusted to keep the so aforementioned contract with god and made the decision to flee the monastery after raiding it's richly lined coffers, sailing for the new world and a fresh start.

Brother Hawley saw it as the lesser of the two evils.

It seemed providence smiled upon Jonathan Hawley and his companions, as the fortune they were able to pilfer away from the corrupt church was much larger than they had initially anticipated. It sickened

WESTING

him to know that such wealth had been hoarded when so many were suffering, taking it had been made easy in that regard. However brother Hawley saw the temptation the gold could bring into their congregation almost from the very start. He determined that he and his fellow conspirators Levi and Abernathy should keep the fortune secret from the rest of their group, having seen all too closely what wickedness greed and power could arise in the hearts of men.

Before Gary could translate any further he realized it was almost around the time Mrs. Culligan would be arriving and so he closed up the two books and went out to his car to stash them. He wasn't stealing pre say, just bringing the volumes home to translate further. Besides it gave him a reason to go outside and stretch his legs, which had begun to fall asleep from sitting most of the night.

Gary had noticed that ever since he slept in his backseat during his dereliction he'd had the problem of leg cramps and the feeling of pins and needles within his lower extremities. Unfortunately it had stuck around after he'd found himself his own bed again and Gary highly doubted he'd ever be rid of it.

He began to walk back towards the library after tucking away the volumes in his backseat when he noticed what looked like someone move inside of the darkened building. It was hard to focus on the interior at first but then he saw it, if only for a second. Ice shot through his veins. Gary thought about running back to his car and driving away, he knew what his eyes had seen but wouldn't let himself believe it.

He needed this job.

WESTING

This opportunity.

He knew that he wouldn't get another.

He had a bed to sleep in and food in his belly, he had a way to get on his feet and out from the charity of his father and he wasn't going to let a reflection off of the hundreds of years old glass make him throw all of that away. It could have been a trick of the lights through the assuredly warped pane. "It was just a reflection." A reflection that had seemed to be peering out of the darkness staring at him with unblinking eyes.

A face.

"Get ahold of yourself. You're just exhausted from changing over to the night shift. If anyone is in that library you're going to get them out or the police will. It's your job. Do your job." Gary bolstered his will, then thought of the line of locals that had been waiting just outside of the mayor's office after his interview; then about the sheriff's comments.

"That's probably it. Someone's trying to scare me out of a job?"

Gary steadied himself but let his anger, which he kept buried inside at all times, wash over him in a wave. "It probably is just someone trying to get me fired. If it's a fight they want, then they picked the wrong guy." He was fuming mad at the thought of it, absolutely furious. Gary walked quickly to the trunk of his car and retrieved his trusty wooden baseball bat, turning its solid weight over in his hands. The weapon felt right between his fingers, wicked, violent, empowering; it's girth emboldening Gary further.

He slammed the trunk and stormed back towards the building with fury in his heart and hatred in his step, measuring the heft of the bat in his hands by tapping it into his palm. No one was going to take his job without a fight. "Let them try it. Just let someone try it."

Gary burst through the arched front door and into the main entrance, bat at the ready. If anyone had indeed tried to pounce on him at that moment Gary had been poised to throttle them to kingdom come with his trusty old slugger. "If you're in here you'd better get out before I catch you!" Gary screamed, trying his best to sound intimidating but no one was there. The library was completely silent and all Gary heard was his own echo by way of any response.

He flicked on the lights and locked the door behind him.

Tap.

Tap.

Tap.

Gary tapped the bat against the door.

WESTING

The place looked empty but Gary still didn't let down his guard. He silently stalked through the packed rows of endless books towards the back of the building and the basement door, searching for any intruders. The building was hushed, quiet enough that Gary could hear a fly ramming into the fluorescent tubes five feet above his head. Every single one of his footsteps on the squeaky tile floor rang out like a gunshot in the silence.

"There'd better be no one here but me!"

The basement door was still locked. Gary checked it twice just to be sure, tapping his key against it three times to again imprint the fact in his mind.

Tap.

Tap.

Tap.

Satisfied, he made his way back to the front and up the stairs to the second floor. Gary was genuinely angry now, something that he'd always struggled with. He'd hated his temper and his enjoyment of violence but it was always a part of who he was. That, like his drinking, he'd inherited from his mother. And in moments where violence was inevitable, her cruel streak came through in Gary clear as day.

WESTING

Even if he didn't want it to.

Bat at the ready, Gary searched through the deserted isles. Peering through the rows apt to pummel any local who'd come to try and scare him off or get him fired. In that moment Gary was ready to teach someone a lesson about trying the thoroughness of his reformation.

He wasn't all the way yet any saint.

After checking the entirety of the second floor twice over, Gary concluded there was no one else there.

But he'd seen someone…

He was sure of it.

He knew beyond any doubt there had been a person standing inside the building looking out at him from one of the windows.

It had shaken him.

He went back downstairs and checked the commodes, they were empty.

The broom closet was also empty.

No one was there.

WESTING

No one he could see.

Gary made himself more coffee and ate donuts he'd brought from the local bakery Sally's, which besides the rude servers was the only good thing really about Westing he'd decided. It's hard to make an exceptional donut and Sally's donuts were divine. He naturally assumed the sour attitudes of the staff had everything to do with his getting the job at the library; it didn't change his affinity for their confectioneries.

Gary devoured two big Boston creams, savoring every delicious morsel of the perfect pastries. Freshly milk chocolate covered and over filled with velvety, almost pudding like cream; exceptional in both taste and texture. "It's just the late nights, nothing more. You're going to get through this, just try and sleep instead of writing when you get home today." Gary reassured himself in his head, it was all he could do. He didn't however return to his vehicle and instead stashed the bat under his desk within arms reach, just in case.

CHAPTER FOUR: THE SECRETS OF WESTING.

Despite his best efforts, when Gary got home he couldn't sleep. He told himself it was the coffee or his nerves. Instead he lay in his bed with his note pad and pen in hand, continuing the translation of Jonathan Hawley's secret journal. He didn't get more than a few pages transcribed before his eyes grew heavy and the sorrow of his translations caused him to stop. It wasn't long after that Gary found himself falling asleep, the weariness of the prior nights stress finally setting in all at once.

The passages he did translate were about the monk's new congregation made up of his friends and relatives as well as all of the children that they had rescued from the siege. The group sailed across the sea with high hopes. However they all also

When he awoke he promptly wrote them all down.

Gary had found himself in total darkness, but he knew instantly that he wasn't alone. He could hear frantic breathing, coughing and light banging coming from very near him. "Come on! Work you piece of junk!" It was Murray Sax banging his dying headlamp against his hand. The bulb came back on, illuminating him to Gary.

Murray was lost in the black tunnel, surrounded by coal and breathing the soot lined air. His face was beyond filthy and Gary saw panic in his eyes. Murray dug through his pockets to see if they contained anything of use, only coming up with his wallet, a zippo and a handkerchief, which he promptly wrapped around his nose and mouth.

WESTING

"Get up. Don't you give up." Murray scolded him.

Murray got up from the ground and began looking at the floor to see if he could make out his own footprints to follow back out. Discovering what he thought were their faint imprints Murray began hurrying away from Gary down the tunnel off into it's darkened shaft following the trail. Gary watched him go, the tunnel eventually going black as Murray disappeared further off into it's recesses.

Panic set in as Gary tried to will himself to follow after the man, having been engulfed in the tunnel's abyss. It was no use. Try as he might Gary couldn't make his limbs obey him, even the sensation of them had disappeared much like Murray's light.

Again Gary felt as he had after he had struck the

match and seen the faces, as if those same horrors were surrounding him in the dark. Then something pulled him, violently flinging his form through the void; propelling him out into a dense half lit forest.

When his voyage ended Gary was in front of Herbert's home again, this time it had a new car parked next to the sheriff's and there was another man standing in front of Herbert's door. Gary hovered a foot off the ground at the edge of the lawn, the eyes of every garden gnome it's overgrown frontage contained were upon him. Gary felt very distinctly that he'd been dreaming and tried to wake himself up, knowing that something in Herbert's house was watching him as well, something far worse than the gnomes.

Gary knew he was having a nightmare.

WESTING

All he wanted was to wake up.

In spite of his best efforts, Gary stayed asleep. In the dream he was forced against his will to float over to the man and observe his every move. The yard gnomes were all staring at Gary as he levitated past them, their bodies slowly turning to follow him. It was both surreal and ultra real to Gary. Like watching a movie in 3D with ones eyelids removed so as to be unable to look away. In fact try as he might Gary close his eyes.

"Wake up Gary. Please wake up." Gary told himself trying to break free from the trance of sleep.

It was no use.

The man, who Gary instinctively knew was Neil Glixson, pounded on the door. Neil seemed upset and Gary knew why, he knew a great deal about the man as his thoughts filtered into his mind; as if his deliberations and memories were both of theirs. Neil was coming for the rent money Herbert owed, as it was now overdue.

It was the middle of the day, but the sky was cloudy and dark with deep rumbling thunder. Neil pounded again and cursed, saying, "I'm sorry to have to have it but I do have to have it Herbert! I heard about your wife from the medics down at the bar! Apparently it shook up the sheriff pretty bad too, nobody's seen him since! He in there with you!?! Are you piss drunk, the both of ya's!?! Just pay me and I'll leave you both to it!" Rain started to fall and Gary knew something dreadful was about to happen. The sky opened up and started pouring down, hard, cold and fast; drenching both Gary and Neil.

Bang!

Bang!

Bang!

Neil pounded on the door.

"Open up it's pouring! Open up goddamnit or I'm comin' in! I know you're in there!" Neil shouted as the soaking rain poured from the sky. Neil's phony sympathies eroded almost immediately and he tried the door handle. It opened and he stepped inside.

A wave of putrid rot hung thick in the air, Gary was all too aware of it's source; yet he was unable to do anything to alert Neil of the lurking danger. "Jesus-H-Christ! What in the name of the lord is that goddamn smell!?!" Neil covered his nose with his shirt, flicked on the lights and searched the top floor while Gary floated behind him. Gary knew Neil couldn't see him and although it was dry in the home Gary desperately wished he could go back out into the rain and leave.

He could write the story in the morning without the terror, which was all-consuming. He knew he was dreaming about his newest writing endeavor and it would only enrich his work but something about the dream felt off, too real in fact. It felt to Gary Wettle that he was in actual danger and his panic was only worsened by the fact that try as he might he couldn't shut his eyes or wake himself up.

WESTING

"It's only a dream, dream about something else." Gary tried commanding his sleeping brain to hand back control over the reigns but it was futile, he just couldn't rouse from his paralyzed slumber.

The rain outside was pounding on the cheap tin roof unmercifully as a torrential downpour swept over the land, drowning out almost all other sounds; all but the soft crying seemingly only Gary could discern. Gary struggled to run, to leave, to cry out or wake up; nothing was successful. Neil reached the top of the basement stairs and opened the door, gagging as the stench of the sheriff's rotten corpse filled his lungs, even through his shirt collar. He very nearly vomited.

"Wake up. Please wake up." Gary pleaded to his

subconscious mind, it went unheard or unacknowledged.

The cries abruptly stopped.

Gary could feel it watching them from the basement.

Gary thought for a moment that Neil had heard the soft weeping.

"Son-of-a." Neil swore under his breath and composed himself for a moment before looking again. Next to the sheriff laying on the barren cement floor was a piece of gold. Neil couldn't help himself, he'd seen it and he made up his mind right then and there that he was going to go into the basement.

Gary could hear his thoughts and tried to scream to warn him but again no words would come. Gary could see someone else in the basement, someone Neil Glixson would have fled in mind shattering fear from if he only caught a glimpse of their face. A figure with unblinking eyes watching him, huddled in the corner, shrouded in darkness, lurking in wait.

It was Herbert Scaghill, or at least his animated corpse.

As Neil slowly descended the stairs Gary finally snapped out of the suffocating nightmare to the sound of his alarm blaring.

Beep!

Beep!

Beep!

It was a logical place to pause his writing even though Gary knew instinctively what had happened next. But the ink ribbon on Gary's typewriter was getting low and he needed to get to work. So he got himself up and about, putting the freshly typed pages away with the others in his nightstand's top drawer. The dream hadn't been exciting while he was within its grasp, quite the contrary as Gary had been terrified. Afterwards though, he was grateful for it.

WESTING

"At least it's like it used to be, good and bad I'll take it." Gary was thankful; it'd been a long time since he'd dreamt of one of his stories. Since he was a child he'd done it up until sometime in his late twenties when it had stopped completely. When he'd listened to his ego and desires more than his dreams.

It invigorated him to be back to making work that was inspired instead of contrived. For too long he'd been writing hollow words, even going so far as to convince himself that his dreams weren't actually the basis of his early writings. Deep down he'd known it was a lie, his dreams had been his greatest inspirations when he'd had a taste of success.

Gary knew he was back on the right path. His work coming to life in his dreams for him to harvest during his waking hours had returned. Ideas were coming instinctively when he sat down to type instead of Gary forcing them out onto the page. Even if it cost him a few nights of restful sleep, Gary figured it was worth it in the long run.

"Success is just a collection of good days and hard work."

Gary stopped on his way into the library to pick up two more donuts from Sally's for his shift, jovial about his life as he eagerly waited for his confections at the counter. He rather loved the little corner bakery with it's old style coffee shop d cor, even if the service was terrible. It seemed to Gary that everyone in Westing but himself was miserable. His happiness faded however when he spotted one of the men he'd seen waiting in line to interview at the mayor's office.

WESTING

The gruff looking fellow was sitting languidly in one of the corner booths, smoking a cigarette and reading the paper. Gary tried to turn away before he was spotted but it was too late, they locked eyes. Gary paid for his donuts and left before the man could get up and Gary hoped he'd make it to his car before there could be any sort of confrontation but the short, portly man caught up to him; stopping him just a few feet from his door.

"You're the fella they gave the night job at the library ain't ya?" The man asked with a sore look. "Yup." Gary replied shortly, taking stock of his options. He thought of punching the man if he took another step towards him but he didn't, he kept his distance. "You know why you got the job?" The man snickered coldly. "Luck." Gary shrugged and turned to get into his car.

"The old librarian up there burst into flames. The two fellas who worked night shift saw it happen. They said she went into the attic and came back down on fire. Nobody knows why, police called it an accident. Spontaneous combustion. You got the job because they didn't have a chance of paying anyone from town what they're paying you, I can tell ya that now fella. Every man in town agreed to stand together to require a second man be brought on as well, then you came along and they got ya for cheap." The man quipped.

"If you say so." Gary said as he shrugged and got in his car then drove away, leaving the man standing outside Sally's smoking his cigarette in the cool October air. Gary wondered if any of what he said was true, thinking most likely it wasn't but then remembering how Mrs. Culligan had turned heel and all but fled from the door to the third floor. Also he dwelled on the pile of charred books in the basement.

"He's full of it. Jealous prick. Probably the guy who was trying to mess with me last night. Just leave him alone with his misery, don't join him in it." Gary said to himself as he pulled into the library parking lot, only half believing his own sentiment. It'd been Gary's experience that people were usually at their core only out for themselves, hell he'd been that way himself for most of his life. Something about the way the man had told the story had been convincing, too sure to be a lie.

Gary walked in to find Mrs. Culligan in her usual less than chipper mood. "May I ask what is taking you so long in sorting the books I assigned you in the basement?" Gary didn't immediately answer but decided to simply ask about the rumor he'd just heard rather than endure her certainly prepared speech about her expectations of him.

"Sorry mam, I'm just trying to be thorough. Say, I hope that it isn't true what I've just been told about what happened to the prior librarian? I just heard she burned to death in the library?" Mrs. Culligan's face went frighteningly pale. "I'm afraid that is true Mr. Wettle. I thought the mayor brought that up to you during your interview. Excuse me." Mrs. Culligan walked into her office and closed the door, again Gary heard the lock click behind her.

If there was any doubt in his mind before that Westing was indeed filled with secrets it was certainly erased by that revelation. Spontaneous human combustion seemed about as likely to Gary as his winning the lottery, more than likely someone had killed the prior librarian. Not just killed her, they burned her alive.

"They burned her alive." The phrase stuck in Gary's mind, simple and cruel. He wondered what she had done to deserve such a fate. "She really must have pissed someone off. Old Mrs. Culligan knows something about it she's keeping to herself, maybe that's why she's so scared?" Gary wondered if she'd been there to see it, he thought of asking but then thought better of it.

"That might be a bridge too far. Don't make her want to fire you anymore than she already does." Gary swept then mopped the first floor, cleaning the bathrooms before ascending to the second floor alone to finish his janitorial duties for the evening. He didn't want to admit it to himself but he was already scared to be alone in the building, hell he was scared to go to the second floor alone even with

Mrs. Culligan downstairs in her office.

"It's just a job Gary, just do it and move on." He assured himself that once he had free time that evening he'd start looking for other work. Maybe he'd even send off what he'd written so far and see if his old publisher could give him an advance so he could simply write full time. Gary knew those days were for the moment on hold, he hadn't had anything sell well in years. Certainly not well enough that anyone was going to advance him anything. "It's fine. I'll get myself out of this hole one way or another and be on to better things soon enough." Gary calmed himself down and cleaned the second floor as quickly as possible.

When he finally reached the door leading to the third floor stairwell he noticed charred markings bleeding through the paint ever so slightly on some of the

WESTING

bookshelves beside it. A portion of the ceiling directly overhead had been repainted and a section obviously replaced. A shiver ran down his spine as he saw that the markings looked to be a handprint, burnt into the bookshelf.

Gary imagined what horrible pain it must have been to burn alive. Being even near the spot set him into an internal panic. "Don't focus on the misery, that's only for the page. Just do your job." He reminded himself sternly but in a kind way and hurriedly finished his mopping, briskly making his way back downstairs. More and more Gary was inclined to believe that after this new book his writing would take on a much less horrific tone.

After so much terror in his life he was ready for other things. As he put away the mop and bucket he dreamed of sailing on a fishing boat with his children, a pleasant enough distraction from the morbid history of his new place of employment. "Fresh crabs and salmon on the beach with the kids sounds about perfect." The idea brought a smile to his face. A vacation spot, or even better a vacation home right on the beach they could visit every winter. It was a pleasant dream, pleasant enough that Gary was shaken out of it by the door to Mrs. Culligan's office opening.

"Have a good evening Mr. Wettle, no sleeping or visitors of course." She spoke, trying her best to sound domineering but Gary could tell she was afraid. Her tone no longer sure. "Of course, I hope you have a lovely evening as well Mrs. Culligan; drive safe!" Gary replied, a smile of genuine joy across his lips.

Gary knew fear, he could smell it like a shark to

blood. Try as she might to humiliate him, it was meaningless if he could scare her. Mrs. Culligan left with her head bowed as if in defeat. Gary felt a small gleam of pride, she was afraid. She'd simply left her office and locked it, then walked out the front door after muttering, "See you in the morning." Without remembering to lock the outside door behind her.

He'd scared her.

It was something that Gary loved to do, even as a young boy. "Maybe you should stop that Gary, it's not nice and it makes you no better than a common bully. Now you've got to hope she doesn't want to actually fire you." Gary wondered then if Mrs. Culligan not locking the front door was a test to see if he'd forget before going downstairs, the upside was he'd noticed.

The downside was that now Gary was alone and had to go into the basement. He locked the door, tapping on it three times with his key to remind himself it was done.

Tap.

Tap.

Tap.

"One. Two. Three. It's locked at 8:03." Then Gary headed downstairs to sort the salvage piles as quickly as possible. "I'll have to finish up fast so the old bag doesn't try and use it as an excuse to write me up. Just keep your head about you Gary, no need to worry it's not that big of a job and you're going to be quick." He told himself. The honest truth was Gary was terrified of being down there alone, now that he had some idea of where the burnt piles of books in the corner of the cellar were from.

Nonetheless Gary sorted through the books faster than before, first putting all that were salvageable into a single pile regardless of their language or subject matter. He was then left with the water damaged and disintegrating volumes covering most of the rest of the floor.

"I'll get to that tomorrow night. When she peeks down here in the morning it'll look like I put at least a sizable dent into it. Hopefully by the time she's figured out nothing's sorted in any real way I'll be gainfully employed elsewhere." Gary smiled to himself as he made his way from the basement, in decidedly better spirits than when he'd come down. Hard work did that for Gary, it refocused him. He knew he'd more likely than not be working at the library for a long time, that didn't mean he couldn't dream of leaving it.

"She's got no cause to fire me. I'm doing everything I'm told and being polite as pie." Polite as pie was one of his mother's favorite sayings and ironically it really meant fake-to-your-face, something his mother had excelled at. Sure she was terrible and sadistic to him behind closed doors but polite as pie whenever they had company over or went out in public.

Tap.

WESTING

Tap.

Tap.

After locking the basement stairwell Gary tapped his key three times on the door, again making a mental note that indeed he had locked it. The habit lent itself to Gary's new found self control, he was creating better patterns of behavior to foster positive growth in every area of his life. One of the main goals of his self help was to get into a routine of success, honesty and gratitude. New routines were critical to fostering the change.

He finally made it back to his desk and immediately began making himself a fresh pot of coffee, having lusted after the donuts from Sally's his entire shift up to that point. The deep roasted aroma of the beans perfumed the air, the fresh brew would be the perfect compliment to his order from Sally's, another bright spot in his life he noted.

"Little things do make all of the difference." Gary smiled at his childlike enthusiasm over fried dough and bean juice. "They might be simple but is there really anything more wonderful?" Gary thought while enjoying the sight of them. His grandfather loved coffee and donuts. Every morning Gary would spend over his grandparent's house for the holidays as a child, his grandfather would bring home a huge box of fresh donuts. Gary had loved them deeply ever since, especially his grandpa's favorite; Boston creams.

As he waited for the pot to finish brewing Gary went to the bathroom and washed his hands, trying to think of what the title for his current writing project

WESTING

might be. Titles were important Gary knew, artistically it sold the book second only to the cover. All of that was of course nothing compared to how much money you had for promotion or who you knew, Gary didn't have to worry about either of those things since he had neither money nor connections.

But Gary knew deep in his heart that writing was in the end an even playing field for an artist. There were no financial hurdles to overcome with it like so many other artistic endeavors. Painters have to buy paint, photography requires film, musicians need instruments… A writer simply needs to write. Gary's only path to success was to put words on the page and he was actively doing just that.

He'd scribbled down a few speculative titles but the one that seemed to fit the most was "The Secrets Of Westing." However he wasn't completely sold on it or at all satisfied with it. It sounded a bit too Nancy Drew and while Gary loved those books as a child they weren't what he was trying to emulate. A horror book's title is supposed to impart not only the promise of mystery, blood and terror but also the necessary foreboding. Gary thought his was bland. He'd also toyed with the idea of "The Mine." Or "The Collapse." but really didn't feel like either would make someone pick the book off the shelf. All three honestly sounded generic and boring to him, the kiss of death for any creative work; much less a book.

He was writing horror, the title needed to be simple and ominous.

"Maybe just Westing?"

Gary was sure he'd be writing the portly man from

WESTING

Sally's earlier into his story regardless of the title, maybe even killing him off in a gruesome way early to help buy some of his reader's attention. People wanted blood, no two ways about it. It was a sign of the times Gary supposed but things sure had changed from the horror books of his youth. Gary was trying to steer clear of making his new work too graphic, trying simply to rely on the aspects of fear that left the reader to imagine their own terrors instead of trying to meticulously lay them out or use grotesqueness to inspire it.

"Maybe I won't write him in, I should cut the guy some slack. He's just sore about being broke, I know all about that." Gary also knew he needed to stop dwelling on the little things and that violence was honestly juvenile. People with small minds choosing to ignore all logic and civility and regress in their behavior to the state of neanderthals.

In reality violent people are only idolized by those who don't know any better or those with corrupt judgement. Violence is only appealing to people that haven't known it, imbeciles or those with malicious intentions. True terror is what lays beyond comprehension in the vast expanses of the unknown. Besides, Gary definitely felt that there wasn't any pride he could take in glorifying vile acts for people's entertainment.

Not anymore.

That was the one thing that Gary kept coming back to over and over in his mind. If he'd dreamt up the faces in the darkness on LSD it wasn't the worst things his mind had created. He'd written far more diabolical and degenerate works of fiction hundreds of times over. Dreamed ugly and brutally sadistic nightmares for people to read for enjoyment.

WESTING

What did that make him?

That he had been unleashing worse than his worst nightmare on the world was a terrible truth for Gary to bare.

"Who cares if this is the one to dig me out of this hole or not? At least I can let my children read it without feeling ashamed for once." Gary smiled at the thought. His past several offerings to the literary world had been smut in every sense of the word. Shock based trash that he'd hoped would appeal to the ever-growing underbelly of society in America amidst the early 1970's.

He'd been wrong.

Because in addition to his works having been too extreme for most of the general public, the lowlife thrill seekers weren't buying them either. Perhaps Gary's assumptions about their consumption of seedy works were misplaced due to the nature of the medium. In plainer words, most connoisseurs of filth weren't reading books, they were watching 8mm films or buying dirty or gory magazines.

Imbeciles, mostly juveniles and imbeciles.

Very few people were reading when they could simply tune out and watch the TV or listen to the radio. Gary figured soon enough they'd be jacked into something else for amusement. "Who knows what new way they'll invent for us to escape our lives." Gary lingered on the fact that it might one day

WESTING

be something so powerful that people might not even realize it wasn't real. "Whoever does that will have quite the legacy." Gary thought.

Legacy and power.

Gary wasn't feeling good about his legacy and although that may sound trivial to a great many people, it had started to dawn on Gary that he didn't have forever left to leave one. Perhaps it was because of his obsession with writing about grisly murders, which had spanned so many years. Perhaps it was living out of garbage cans or off the charity of a cruel world. Perhaps it was what he saw in the darkness after his campfire had died. Regardless Gary had been thinking more and more about what he'd leave behind when it was indeed his time to go and he was less than enthusiastic about the current state of his work and life's imprint.

"We're like ripples through water, spreading out across the entire face; touching everything in our path." Gary mused as he shut off the percolator which was dripping the last drops of the boiling hot water to steep through the finely ground beans. Gary filled his lungs with the aroma as he watched it brew. The pot finished and Gary took it off as soon as the last drop fell, making sure to first pour in the creamer so he could get his color perfect every time. Four sugars, Gary liked his coffee sweet and creamy.

"These things are important." Gary chuckled to himself.

The coffee was divine. Gary scarfed down the first donut while savoring the hot liquid in-between bites, perfectly washing down the velvety Boston creams. Sally's sure knew how to make the perfect donut, though Gary would now think twice about going in there ever again.

Gary corrected his dismal self loathing quickly. "No. It's no big deal. Just like this job. Don't take everything so personally. Stop letting little things trip you up. Of course the local prick who feels like you stole his shot at a job is going to give you a hard time, don't let him. One day soon this place will be a distant memory, something you'll tell interviewers about when they ask what inspired your work. If that prick doesn't stop trying be the tough guy he'll be stuck at the donut shop, trying to bully his way into some other low-end job. You worry about you."

Gary began to feel better about things and resolved to go back tomorrow for another round of the scrumptious morsels. "To hell with it, I don't care what they say or think about me. Why should I? I'm the one they hired. I'm the only one who probably was qualified to actually do the job. I doubt half of the doofuses in that line know how to read above a fifth grade level, much less name a single current author. I even felt empathy for them when I got the job and never wished them any ill will. I'm doing the right things and I just want to be better than to have enemies. If anyone tries to give me trouble all I have to do is let them keep it."

Gary smiled to himself and sat down to finish his second donut. "As far as this place, just remember, you're the one who scares people." His mental pep talk went a long way in calming him and soon Gary was again lost in his work translating the journal, filled by the coffee and donuts along with his conviction that indeed his ambitions would bare fruit.

WESTING

Believing everything would turn out right was one of the things Gary was trying to work on in his life, his self help books called it positive manifestation. He liked to believe they were right, at least the concept seemed to make sense. When he'd enjoyed some manner of success he'd never doubted it would come, rather he'd expected it to. It was only when Gary got sloppy and stopped caring that things fell apart. He'd stopped writing for the joy of it and instead was purely doing it for the perks that it brought, seeking attention for his own ego. The ability to pick up women who would never have looked twice at him for example.

It wasn't that Gary had ever been ugly but he didn't consider himself good looking either, just plain. But if he told a beautiful woman at the bar he was a published author, or they happened to come to one of his book signings well; they started looking at him differently. Deep down he knew they weren't really attracted to anything more than the promise of money and fame but he didn't split hairs on the why of their attentions or affections, nor could he refuse them. That was the start of it all crumbling. His life, work, family, home, ambition…

"Just do your work." He kept telling himself. "This place is the perfect set up for a scary story. All you have to do is focus and you'll be able to make something great, something that'll make your life better. Stop worrying about all the things that won't help you because they'll only drag you down." Gary renewed his translation with vigor, ready to make something of himself again.

The journal of brother Jonathan Hawley took back up as the monk and his brethren journeyed across the sea. Seventy-two days across the open ocean. Gary wondered what that must have been like, adrift in the middle of the sea with no land anywhere in sight,

WESTING

at the mercy of the captain's word and the will of nature. Brother Hawley wrote that along with the orphans many of his congregation perished from illness during the voyage and had to be buried at sea, the risk of keeping their corpses on board was too great for fear of spreading the contagion.

Gary thought about the resolve of Jonathan Hawley and how unyielding it truly had to have been. To have risked being put to death if his theft was discovered then undertaken such a perilous journey to an unknown land were reason enough to admire him. What really struck Gary was his ability to see the beauty in simple things. One of the passages in his journal regarding the voyage across the sea described the sheer splendor of the stars at night over the open ocean. Gary thought that he could learn a lot from such a sentiment when confronting his own life's obstacles.

"Just remember to look at the stars old boy. They're always there so don't take them for granted." Gary filled another mug with coffee, making sure the cream and sugar ratios were again just right. He sipped the steeping hot brew trying to rejuvenate himself before returning to his translation.

After landing in the established English colony of Providence, the very name of which Jonathan Hawley took to be a sign of good fortune for his congregation; they set out to establish their own settlement. One far beyond any already in existence so as to avoid detection by those who may come seeking. The congregation bought supplies, horses and oxen; constructing a wagon train with which they could transport their newly acquired provisions. The journal explained their struggles trekking through the dense forest in great detail and then of the congregation's establishment of a new settlement within the deep wilderness at a place the local tribes had avoided in spite of it's seemingly

WESTING

perfect geographical trappings.

Westing.

Gary hated religiously obsessive thinking and every other sentence from the monk was either a reference to god or thanking him for one thing or another. But even Gary had to admit that the monk had good reason to be thankful. Not only was Jonathan Hawley able to escape from a civil war and then travel across an ocean to a new land, he had managed to keep a large portion of the people who set out with him alive and his treasure a secret.

Gary dreamt of being among them as they made their way through the unknown forests and came to the very spot he now sat overlooking the valley within which they had built Westing. How perfect it must have seemed surrounded by natural barriers and filled with lush fields fed by mountain springs and before Gary knew it; he looked at the clock and it was almost time for him to head home.

When Mrs. Culligan arrived she barely said hello to Gary, he worried that perhaps he'd gone too far asking about the prior librarian. However when a homeless drifter attempted to enter the library, she addressed Gary as if nothing had happened. It pained Gary terribly to have to stand by her as she ran the man off, knowing exactly how he felt. Gary was able to keep his feelings bottled up, even as Mrs. Culligan went on a tirade after the poor man was gone about how, "Men like that shouldn't be allowed in public places until they've cleaned themselves up."

Men like Gary had been.

WESTING

"They use the bathroom here to wash. Just pathetic. I can't stand it when they come in, the smell is terrible. The sheriff won't do anything either unless it's after hours. That wretched bum will be back as soon as we're open again and won't leave every day until we close, stinking up the place. Supposedly it's his right, so I've got to babysit a grown man all day and make sure he doesn't steal anything." Mrs. Culligan's tone was pure contempt and Gary, much to his own disgust, found himself agreeing with her out of fear of losing his own job.

If she only knew who he had been.

The drive home he wept. Looking around the whole way to see if he could spot the poor man on any of the benches or walking the streets into town. He didn't know what he'd do if he did spot him, perhaps give him what little change he had in his pockets or offer him the blanket he still had tucked in his trunk; maybe even buy him a meal. The fall air had turned cold that morning and Gary knew all too well the desperation that went along with the seasons change when you had nowhere to call home.

Gary didn't see the man and as he pulled up to his apartment he sat a few moments in his car to calm himself. "He'll be alright. He probably walked back to the freeway and moved on to the next town. You're not a bad person for doing what you needed to do so that you're ok. Your kids need you to be. You need this job." Gary went inside to cook himself a simple meal of spaghetti and sauce. It felt strange to be taking his dinner when most people were eating breakfast but Gary supposed he'd have to get used to it at least for the time being. He'd forgotten to pick up a newspaper or an ink ribbon on his way home. That meant Gary couldn't search the want ads or

WESTING

type his stories but he didn't feel like he needed to beat himself up anymore than he already had so he sat silently and enjoyed the spaghetti.

The trick to good sauce is to saut the onions and garlic with meat before you add in the tomatoes, letting it simmer together for as long as possible; saving the fresh lemon juice and basil for the very end.

Gary savored the pasta, grateful to have the hot food. Grateful for the warmth of it and the joy he felt at the excellent flavor as he consumed it. Gary wasn't anything close to as good a cook as his grandmother had been; his sauce wasn't nearly as rich or complex. Still, Gary prided himself on his homemade marinara, with fresh garlic and lemon juice. He'd even got fresh parsley and good parmigiana to finish it off, impressive; even if the meal was somewhat barren without meatballs.

"Small victories Gary, that's all life really is." He reminded himself that things weren't bad, he wasn't finished with his meal before the pull to write was tugging at him more than his gut. "Slow down, enjoy this first." He reminded himself. After all it wasn't long ago he'd have given anything for what he currently had. A hot meal. A roof to eat it under. Each bite reminded Gary that indeed he had turned things around and that his future was literally his to write.

It's impossible to properly convey the complexity of a writer's self-deprecation. Quite often finding oneself locked in a standstill over a single word or unluckier still, an idea. Beating yourself up over every line, constantly feeling like giving up or to do nothing at all. The pull to do nothing was strong with Gary, as it

WESTING

is with almost all writers or any dreamer. Excuses are everywhere and most people take them.

You can only be successful as a creative person by being creative and sometimes that can't be forced, but it can be realized always through constant determination and making the most out of one's limitations. Limitations are the roadmaps to success, or so Gary had read in his self-help books. Besides, Gary had time alone to work and knew he'd be a fool not to.

Time alone is the ultimate creative tool. The more time you have without any disturbances to focus on any work, the better you can refine it. Artists who can focus themselves inwards on their craft rather than being tempted by the lures of the outside world which only serves as a distraction, will hone their skills and instead of indulging escapism; create it.

As someone brilliant once said, you are either the dreamer or dreaming someone else's dream.

"I'm the dreamer." He reminded himself.

Gary's ink ribbon was all but dry and instead of getting down or giving up Gary took his pen and pad out and renewed his translation of the journal. After all he was imagining that even if the story of brother Hawley and the early years of Westing as a settlement were just a small portion of his own larger narrative about the town; he was indeed planning on using it. Having a backstory was something that even if he didn't touch upon it at all, he figured would only strengthen and enrich the plot. Besides, it was an amazing story to imagine and Gary knew that was the type of story people wanted to read.

WESTING

Gary fantasized what it must have been like to have built the settlement from nothing in the deep wilderness. Clearing trees and brush, tilling fields and sowing them. He admired the monk and his congregation for their resolve. Not only was the labor back breaking, the very real coming of the next winter threatened to freeze them all dead. Hacking down timber, laying foundations, making their clothes a stitch at a time; all with little more than hand tools and a few beasts to lessen the tremendous burden sounded like an enormous task. Especially so terribly isolated from everything and all that the congregation had ever known.

Gary's favorite passages were about the men hunting wild deer and feasting on their bounty when they first arrived in the valley that would become Westing. A joyful celebration of the promise of great things to come, where the entire congregation stood together around a large bonfire sharing the fresh venison. They danced long into the night as they sang songs of praise. That first night had been deceptively joyful as most everyone agreed that the land was an ideal spot to make their settlement.

That impression would certainly sour.

They'd set out in early spring but all too quickly the seasons changed and the rain soaked rebirth of the world ripened into long, sweltering days. All the while the men and women of brother Jonathan Hawley's congregation endured the dreadful biting flies and numerous poisonous snakes, which inhabited the land.

After months of toiling in the oppressive summer heat the congregation had erected homesteads for

WESTING

all who'd survived the voyage, a forge, a mill and even a grand church to worship in. Something that was the first to cause ire amongst some of the settlement. More than a few of the flock still held onto their puritan beliefs that the church was to be a simple place, not a humongous building towering over the entire village up on the furthest ridge.

Brother Hawley quelled the outcry by explaining that the church would have to double as the congregation's stronghold should there be any tribulations that might arise and that in fact, all were welcome to use the church as their own at all times. It stood guard over all of the homesteads below it in the valley and although they hadn't encountered any hostile visitors; it still stood to reason that indeed they might.

It seemed for the time being most of the flock were

happy with the explanation and many even rejoiced at the thought of being able to utilize the grand construction without impediment. There were still some amongst them those who had doubts but they held their tongues everywhere except behind closed doors. Jonathan Hawley was a man with a vision and will, which was undeniable to those within his flock.

With the stolen gold brother Hawley was also able procure supplies enough from the nearest settlement to hold his congregation over through the bitter winter. There would be meats and grains, dried fruits and nuts enough to fill their stores. Extra goats and chickens to sustain them in a pinch. Brother Hawley was optimistic that they wouldn't need to dip into the rations unless absolutely necessary, hoping that his flock wouldn't become indulgent and lazy from the bounty.

WESTING

Gary tried to imagine plucking every feather from a chicken before cooking it and was grateful that he'd grown up not having to. Even with all the gold in the world it wouldn't have made much difference when brother Hawley was alive, especially in his situation; you'd have to butcher your own meat. Gary thought about having a fortune that one couldn't easily spend, as well as a bounty upon one's head.

That's why the construction of a secret furnace was critical. With the furnace brother Hawley and his conspirators were able to melt the gold down before trading it, so that no one had yet caught onto their dubious theft. In fact the greatest threat to the settlement's secret treasure came from inside the settlement itself.

Levi and Abernathy.

His coconspirators wanted to melt the entirety of the fortune down immediately but brother Hawley wouldn't hear of it, knowing that once the coins were made into raw bars his ability to keep watch over it would vanish. Presently he was the only one who knew of it's whereabouts and he agreed only to melt a small portion of the treasure at a time, as needed. Dividing it evenly amongst himself for the settlement and his two now, less than trusted allies.

Jonathan Hawley was more worried by the day about the other men he'd recruited to help him lead the congregation. Their constant insistence that they should spend more of the ill-gotten wealth was growing ever more sinister in tone. Levi and Abernathy were of the mind that they should invest as much of the gold as quickly as possible to give themselves and the settlement a strong foundation. A thinly veiled lie that even they plainly didn't seem

WESTING

to believe.

They only wanted more for themselves.

Seeing through the men's greed Jonathan Hawley proposed to live frugally for as long as possible. Posturing that they shouldn't do anything that would arouse suspicion from their neighbors who might pass the story of a rogue settlement, rich with gold; onto anyone else with whom they traded.

The church would surely be looking for them and for all the mercy they preached each Sunday, if they discovered the thieves there would be none. Brother Hawley also insisted they needed to remain frugal to preserve the fortune for their settlement's future, should a time of great need befall them. Levi and Abernathy didn't seem swayed but were temporarily quelled when brother Hawley agreed to melt down a bit more gold to add to their own current portions.

Jonathan Hawley tried to reason then with the men, begging them not to spend it excessively. There were those among their own flock who would most certainly have thought differently about their supposed leadership's purity if they were to uncover any measure of the truth. Brother Hawley knew that his people weren't blind, especially living in such isolation and proximity.

As the harsh Pennsylvania winter fell upon the land around them that first year, Jonathan Hawley's worries were confirmed. His once trusted and loyal childhood friends, Levi and Abernathy; set out without his blessing or consent to buy unnecessary comforts with the extra portion of melted gold he'd entrusted them. This immediately spread discord and unrest amongst the rest of the settlement, as the two men obviously had come back with much more than they should have been able to trade for on their meager harvests.

Levi and Abernathy had set out alone and bought themselves oxen, cattle and sheep, fine clothes and even secretly spirits, which brother Hawley had forbidden within the settlement. They'd made trades with Spanish settlers from the neighboring colony and assured Jonathan he needn't worry, as the Spaniards hated the British crown. When brother Hawley brought up the building unease and distrust within the settlement the two men brushed it off, assuring him they'd be able to explain it as a loan from the men they'd traded with.

Levi and Abernathy's greed and indulgences so fervently stirred up the curiosities and ire within the rest of the congregation, that brother Hawley was forced to lie further and produce more gold to satisfy his now incessant flock. Jonathan of course evenly distributed his portion of gold amongst the rest of the settlement, allowing everyone to buy oxen, grain and extra winter provisions even though they weren't in any need. He told the congregation that they'd found gold in the hills of Westing, a boldfaced lie.

The rest of the Westing settlement then sent their own party of men to go trade with the Spanish. After they made it to the colony and conducted their trades, amongst which certainly were copious amounts of liquor; they headed back towards their new found home rich with trinkets and the spoils of their visit with the Spanish merchants and tradesmen.

The liquor was hardily consumed on the party's first

night alone on the way back to the settlement around their nights fire. The men were merry and satisfied with themselves and their newfound wealth, discussing what plans they had for their new lands and their families. After a full and hearty meal of fresh goat all indulged in the rum the Spaniards had shipped in from distant tropical shores.

All seemed pleasant enough as the men drank their fill of the sweet sugary liquor until the deep night came on and it was time to extinguish the fire and tuck in. That's when they heard her, somewhere far off in the deep woods; screaming. Her calls for help were almost mistaken for an animal by the men who didn't know how or why anyone would be alone in that isolated wilderness. They were also afraid of what they knew of the legends of witches, who supposedly lured men to their deaths in the forests.

There were several pages torn out of the journal at that point and Gary frustratingly thought that whatever these pages must have contained were certainly the most important, because of the plain and simple fact that the rest of the journal contained more than one truly damning secret brother Jonathan Hawley certainly didn't want known to the world. Gary flipped through the remaining pages and noticed a portion was also missing from the end of the text. However, there were several more pages past the missing chunk that he could translate. Frustrated but determined Gary returned to his work.

Brother Hawley had come to the new world to flee the excesses and sins he so plainly saw amongst the leaders of his church back in England, now, despite his best efforts; he found himself embroiled within their grasp and entangled himself in the very deceptions he had found at the vile heart of his former masters.

WESTING

Corruption had come into the settlement of Westing and regardless of how much he hated to admit it even to himself, Jonathan Hawley knew he was the root of the cause. Brother Hawley decided to take matters into his own hands and buried the remaining treasure where he knew his compatriots wouldn't ever find it, removing it's temptation. His diary gave no clue as to where and the last lines within it's pages only were filled with prayers for forgiveness and a fresh start from the lord.

Gary put down the book and thought about the connection his mind had made between the diary and the text on the riots of Westing, astonished by his discovery he was thrilled to think of it's implications beyond the context of a simple research project. The mob had killed Jonathan Hawley along with Levi and Abernathy, their stolen treasure was never recovered.

Not only did Westing have a great secret, it had a great treasure. It was also not lost on Gary that his own writing as well as dreams seemed in line with these revaluations. Gary brushed it aside as coincidence. "Maybe they were inspired by the journal subconsciously." He reasoned. In his mind surely they could be nothing more. People can go to the greatest lengths to rationalize the irrational or normalize a truly glaring sign that something isn't right. Most will try their hardest to explain away the unexplainable.

Deny it and you don't have to confront it.

Gary, still on fresh legs from his campfire LSD experience rationalized everything as coincidental or illogical, even magical thinking on his own part. The image of his own campfire experience had immediately assailed him upon translating the settlers. It turned his veins to ice. Empathy can certainly prolong trauma.

The eyes watching him.

He had to stop thinking of it. "Stop, it's over and you're ok. That wasn't real, it was the drugs you took when you were alone at a low point in your life. What you saw was a hallucination. Even if it wasn't and it was a lesson about changing your life you've learned it so just move on. Don't dwell on it." Gary tried to focus on the good things he now had in life as he put away his pad and pen to go clean up the dishes.

Dinner had been delicious and Gary was tired, he

had his own bed to sleep in. No small comfort even if it was too small. Gary reminded himself to be thankful and felt sure sleep would set him right. After washing all the dishes, pots and silverware and putting everything away Gary lay down in his undersized bed and passed out. The breeze blowing over his exposed feet being a tad bit cold was the last thing he felt before sleep took him.

CHAPTER FIVE: LIFE IMITATES ART.

Gary's feet were freezing and stuck in what felt like wet, stony earth. He found himself immobilized, enshrouded in darkness. Choked, coughing sobs echoed closer and closer from within the blackened space. Gary could taste the soot hanging in the air with each breath and it wasn't long before he began hacking out of control himself. There was an all-consuming single thought that kept repeating in

WESTING

Gary's mind, although Gary knew it wasn't his own. "If I could only see the ground I could follow my footsteps out."

Gary knew the origin of the thoughts, they belonged to Murray Sax and he was panicking. Illogical. Desperate. His next thought was terrifying to Gary, it was crystal clear and insane.

"I have a lighter."

Scht…

The sound of metal striking flint without sparking sent Gary off, he screamed at the top of his suffocated lungs but not a whimper came out. Gary knew that an open flame within the soot filled chamber would mean death.

Scht…

The flint struck again. Nothing.

"Please work I just need to see the floor!"

Gary tried to grab hold of Murray in the dark but it was no use, he couldn't find him in time.

Schhhhhhhht….

WESTING

The explosion was instantaneous after the lighter threw sparks into the coal shaft. Millions of particles bursting into flame at once, filling the chamber and catapulting Gary away from the blast.

Cold air suddenly rushed over his entire body and instead of being engulfed in flames Gary felt himself flung through the clouds across what felt like a very great distance. He wasn't flying, rather he was rocketing through the sky. Gary's body felt weightless and his propulsion through the aether was more akin to him being pulled at great speed than flight. All at once Gary came to an abrupt halt in the middle of Westing's more upscale residential section at the bottom of a hill.

Even in this part of town Gary saw that almost all of the once luxurious mansions that had housed the mine's prestigious owners and management now stood boarded up and falling to ruin. The blight of beautiful homes, which had sunk into general disrepair, was everywhere Gary looked. Most of the once grand structures having been poorly converted and portioned off into cheap rental properties, if not just lying vacant entirely as the majority did.

Gary slowly floated up the desolate street towards a large plush home at the top of the hill. This house stood apart from the others in that it's splendor hadn't yet gone to ruin like the rest of the buildings in Westing. It's tall hedges were beautifully trimmed and shaped. The shrubberies surrounding a still proud mansion, shielding it from the otherwise poverty stricken street. The grandiose building was the last truly magnificent home in Westing. A monument to the greed of it's owner.

It also happened to be Neil Glixson's house, Herbert

WESTING

Scaghill's landlord. Neil owned most of what was worth owning in Westing, having inherited it from his father who'd shrewdly bought up large portions of the town when the mine closed.

Gary floated up to the front door over the tops of the hedges, looking down upon their spire tips as he passed them over. The front lawn was immaculately trimmed and the front door itself adorned with a large brass doorknob in the shape of a lion.

Gary turned the handle and the door opened easily. His interaction with physical world seemed unreal, the door hadn't made any noise at all when he'd opened it or closed it behind him. Almost as if he was muted. When he entered the home Gary saw Neil sitting alone at his kitchen table with all of the window shades drawn. On the table in front of Neil was a pile of gold coins mounded up high enough to be almost spilling over onto the floor.

Neil Glixson lived alone as he had his entire adult life, one of the most despised people in all of Westing as his father had been before him. The Glixson family were notorious misers with their wealth, unwilling to let anyone slide on even the smallest of debts to them. It'd been that way in Westing since the mine opened and the Glixson's were given the construction contract on all of the residential homes to be built for the staff and had only gotten worse.

The Glixson's were leaches; it was something Neil took pride in. Bleeding the town slowly after it had sunk into it's economic ruin the Glixson's had accumulated most of the deeds for themselves, Neil had planned to take his father's advice and sell out to a developer once the opportunity presented itself.

WESTING

With his father dead the profits would be all Neil's to reap but no one had any interest in buying. Westing was too out of the way to be a potential tourist spot and too shoddy to market as a vacation destination.

None of that mattered any longer to Neil.

Gary floated around the table, his feet hovering just above the floor. He noticed how truly disgusting Neil was as a man, even living in such a well furnished and maintained home. Neil's grin was stained brown from years of neglect and his hygiene was abysmal, Gary could smell the man's reek from ten feet away. His hair was matted to his head with gel that hadn't been washed out in a week or more. His clothes stunk of his reek even though they'd been freshly washed at the Laundromat before he put them on.

Gary could also read his thoughts. It felt vile to be inside the man's mind but Gary couldn't help himself, it was as if their brains synced to the same frequency; only Gary was positive Neil couldn't detect the union. The majority of Neil's ponderings were depraved fantasies he entertained for his newfound fortune, however some were memories of vile things Neil had done with his life and wealth over the years. He was fondly comparing the two in his mind. Neil Glixson was the type of man Gary had written about many, many times in his darkest days. A man with a taste for the misery of others.

A ruiner.

Gary knew exactly what Neil planned to do with the gold. He had decided to take it into Harrisburg where Neil knew a less than reputable pawn store owner named George McCullen. He had arranged with

WESTING

George to move the gold and for his percentage help Neil launder it, no questions asked. He'd gone to see George first thing after taking the fortune from the Skaghill's basement where he found it half hidden by a tarp and covered in Herbert's brains.

Washing every gold piece in triplicate had taken Neil some time but he'd spent it happier than he could remember, regardless of the horrific task. He'd been alone for hours in the Skaghill's basement hard at work while the storm raged outside, making sure every piece of his treasure was shining. Neil had already been rich by Westing standards, now he was rich by any standard. He didn't even mind the sheriff's corpse laying on the floor behind him, the dead man's eyes watching his every move as he huddled over the filthy sink scrubbing the coins.

Once or twice Neil had felt as though the dead

sheriff were standing behind him while he polished his spoils, the feeling had been strikingly palpable but each time Neil had turned to see Jeremiah's corpse unmoved.

Neil planned on selling the properties he owned in Westing regardless of the profits then to move down south where he would ride out his remaining days living the easy life. Plenty of sunshine and relaxing, without any deadbeat hillbilly tenants that destroyed his properties and were always late on their rent. He just couldn't wait to feel the Florida breeze on his face, he planned on getting a new Cadillac of course; something with all the options.

Maybe he'd even buy himself an old orange orchard just to give himself enough space. Neil was smiling from ear to ear as he daydreamed over the pile of shining gold coins glittering in the few rays of the

WESTING

fading sun which had managed to sneak in through the drawn curtains.

Then all at once, Neil froze.

Gary felt the terror radiating off of Neil Glixson in waves.

Someone was watching Neil, someone was in his home.

Gary felt the rooms temperature drop and the air fill with tense electricity. Neil stiffened at the table, his expression no longer jovial but now one of complete fear. Try as hard as he might, Gary found he couldn't turn around and see what Neil was looking at;

although at first Gary thought it was him.

It wasn't.

Gary watched Neil get up from his seat and brandish the gun he had concealed in his lap, taking aim and pointing it off into the darkened living room behind him. "Come on out now, you got nowhere to hide." Neil spoke firmly and cocked the hammer back on the shiny steel weapon, frantically scanning the room for any signs of an intruder. He was terrified. Gary could hear Neil's thoughts racing through his mind…

Neil had seen it.

WESTING

Whatever had been in the basement at the Scaghill's. Neil Glixson had seen it. He'd seen the unearthly face watching him from the darkness of his living room but was convincing himself it must be an intruder who had flesh and blood. Someone after the gold. Maybe he'd been followed, he had felt watched the entire time he'd been in the Skaghill's but just kept brushing it off as nerves and the sheriff's dead eyed stare.

Gary knew better.

Neil had seen it disappear into the darkness but was so disoriented by everything about its appearance that all he could really make out were its eyes. "I know you're there. I can hear you breathing." Neil demanded, advancing past Gary who was frozen in place; his body refusing to move even an inch. Gary could only will his eyes to move and he followed Neil as far as he could with them until Neil moved past him and Gary lost sight of him, disappearing further into the house.

"Go on, come on out now." Gary could hear as Neil tried to sound commanding. It was less than convincing. Gary noticed a mirror hanging next to the front door that showed a reflection of the home behind him. Gary oddly noticed that he himself wasn't within it, though Gary could clearly make out everything around him as well as a slight portion of the dining room behind him. Neil quickly moved out of his sight within the mirror, passing through the dining room further into the massive house beyond.

Gary listened as he heard Neil walk around the home, first stalking through the back portion of the downstairs and then finally making his way upstairs to check for the intruder Gary prayed Neil didn't find.

WESTING

His footsteps seemed to thunder overhead as Gary floated alone in the kitchen unable to move. Gary could hear everything though, including every faint thought and emotion of Neil's as he searched his second floor. Gary caught distinct flashes of what Neil was seeing, almost as if he were being sucked inside Neil's head to observe through his eyes.

The claustrophobia of being held in stasis was beginning to overwhelm Gary. It felt like he was being crushed by his own weight, hanging limp in midair. There was the faintest hint of a fowl odor beginning to permeate the room, the smell of something acrid and vile; burnt and decayed. This odor mixed with the overwhelming, inescapable dread Gary had consuming him. As he tried to calm himself and place the origin of the stench, Gary again heard Neil's thoughts racing through the floorboards.

Neil was running through the list of who he suspected could have snuck into his house. Maybe the temptation was too great and the fence he'd traveled to see earlier had decided to keep everything for himself. "George McCullen wouldn't do anything like that. He may be a crook but he's an honest crook." Neil told himself. "But maybe the person on the other end of the deal had decided to cut themselves in for the whole pie? Who knows who George tried to move the gold onto, it could be anyone for the money and it's no small amount of money." Neil's rationale wasn't illogical but the truth was far worse.

As he checked through all the rooms Neil grew less and less certain about what he'd seen and began to rationalize the entire situation as a mirage. He was tired; he'd been up all night. First he'd had to clean, then transport the gold to his friend George McCullen, give him a sample to tender to his buyer; all while pretending the rest of the fortune wasn't in bags in the trunk of his car while they worked out his cut. He'd had to share 50/50 with the man which in any other situation he hated but Neil knew silence was priceless in devious matters and fairness encouraged it. Neil had to then drive home and compose himself, which meant drinking liquor.

Lots of it.

Neil was drunk as hell by the time the sun came up, too drunk to carry the gold up to his room. So he'd decided to stay with his treasure in the kitchen until the buzz wore off and he could stash it upstairs. It'd been his one last chance to really see the gold before it was gone and Neil was going to take it.

Maybe he'd had a few more drinks than he should have but it had been a celebratory occasion and he had indulged. Neil didn't think that would normally lead to anyone seeing terrifying faces lurking in the shadows but with his excessive drinking coupling with the fact that he had also seen his share of death that morning constituted extenuating circumstances. The sheriff had certainly killed Herbert Scaghill over the treasure, of that Neil was fairly certain.

The blood and gore on the gold hadn't been the sheriff's after all.

Gary heard Neil audibly sigh from upstairs as he finished looking through each room, then Gary heard Neil come sauntering back downstairs. Neil was trying to avoid thinking about the morbid details of his newly acquired fortune, his only ponderings being of hiding it before tucking in for a short nap. He needed to be sharp for the evening's transaction,

WESTING

he trusted George McCullen but he didn't trust money. Neil needed the rest so he could be ready for anything when it was time to make the switch.

Gary watched in the mirror as Neil made his way back to the kitchen table from within the house and began putting the gold coins in his travel bags. He'd used the bags more than once for smuggling heroin into the town of Westing, an operation that had since far overgrown it's profitability. This was no surprise to Neil as by its very nature heroin ruins everyone it touches. He'd stopped dealing it and the bags had sat empty for almost two years in his trunk before Neil used them to bring the gold from the Scaghill's to his kitchen table. The sheriff was of course in on it, Neil had to pass him every time he came into or left town.

"They're going to find the sheriff, dead on a property

I own and come asking questions; don't get sloppy now. You won't be able to spend any of this gold if you're in a cell. And unless you make it very easy for them no one will ever find out about any of it. You'll be down off the coast day fishing wasted on rum." Neil finished putting the gold back into his oversized travel suitcases, which were bulging so badly he had a hard time closing them.

His smile had returned along with his happy daydreams but Gary knew Neil shouldn't feel safe. He wanted to scream out to Neil to run, even as much as Gary despised the man he wished him no ill will. But something in that house did, Gary could sense it. Each moment it was getting closer to striking.

A sinister undercurrent gaining strength with each passing second.

WESTING

Gary remained locked in place as he watched Neil take the heavy bags back upstairs, then listened to him stash them under his bed. He heard as Neil then climbed onto the mattress exhausted but excited, tucking his gun under his pillow and settling in. Gary again tried screaming out to Neil to get out of the house but it was of no use. Neil was oblivious, ready to let sleep take him. Laying face down on his bed's thick comforter with thoughts of beach front property, pi a colada's with a tiny umbrella in them and of course plenty of scantily clad women.

Gary was stuck in place, gripped by his terrible sense of impending dread; it's smothering grasp building towards an unbearable crescendo.

In the mirror Gary saw the door to Neil Glixson's

basement slowly swing itself open with a loud creek, Neil heard it as well even upstairs.

It was the one place he'd forgotten to check.

Neil reached under his pillow and pulled the revolver back out, cocking its hammer. Gary tried repeatedly with all his will to call out to the man to warn him not to come back downstairs. Neil didn't hear him; he was doing exactly the thing Gary was trying so hard to get him not to do. Neil was coming out of his room and heading to check the basement.

"If there is someone here you'd better leave now!" Neil yelled as he stalked back down the stairs, gun at the ready. He was scared out of his mind, Gary shared his feelings and was even more terrified, terrified because he knew what was about to happen. "Get out! Go out the back door! Don't go near the basement!" Gary thought being locked in place, trying his hardest to make any sound or reach Neil through his thoughts. It didn't work. Gary remained completely immobile, unable to influence any part of the world around him.

Neil turned the corner, stepping out into the first floor; appearing in Gary's view in the mirror. He was storming towards the basement, hoping his bravado would intimidate whoever was down in it. Once Neil reached the top of the stairs he stopped and flicked on the cellar lights, hesitating out of primal fear. Neil knew in his gut that he was in danger. Still, he had to deal with whoever had broken into his home and calling the police wasn't an option.

"I'm coming down there so you'd better show yourself with your hands high! This is private property and I am armed with my gun! If you wanna live to see tomorrow you'd better do exactly what I say! Come out! Come out now!" Gary watched as Neil waited at the top of the stairs when the lights blinked out in the basement. They weren't turned out, the bulbs had all burned out at the same time.

Neil froze, Gary sensed his panic. Gary knew he'd seen it again, for a moment when the bulbs burnt out. The eyes staring back at him from the darkness with an unearthly glimmer.

"Fine! I'm locking you in here and calling the sheriff!!!" Neil shouted into the darkened basement in front of him, his voice audibly trembling. Neil went to slam the door when an unseen force pulled him off of his feet, lofting him down the stairs into the basement headfirst. Gary heard Neil screaming as he fell and a wave of terror racked through his body as Neil's thoughts screamed out and blasted into his own.

Neil had indeed seen it again, this time right up close.

A face too terrible to describe.

It was horribly wretched; the eyes were eerily wide boring through him, hanging just over the snarled lips. It was the face of something that once had been human but was now charred beyond recognition. Neil screamed as he fell, trying to pull the trigger on his gun but for some unearthly reason he was unable to. He still held a firm grasp onto the six-shooter as he tumbled down the stairs but he was unsuccessful in all of his many attempts to fire it, try as he might with all of his heart. Tumbling down the stairs only took an instant and Neil didn't even have a moment at the bottom to feel it, slamming his head into the concrete floor. He vanished from Gary's mind on impact and his thoughts went black.

Gary assumed Neil was dead; something about the severing of the connection between their minds felt very much like death to him. Hovering in stasis unable to fly away, Gary tried to will himself out of the room but he still could not. Gary knew he was dreaming but he couldn't wake up. He tried telling himself it was all just a nightmare and that he could simply rouse from it's grasp but it was of no use. Gary couldn't even will his eyes to close. He was wide eyed, paralyzed and terrified.

In the mirror he saw something, at first it gave him comfort but then a wave of shuddersome fear filled Gary to his core. It was Neil Glixson emerging from the darkness of the basement; he'd survived the fall without so much as a scratch on him that Gary could see. There was however something very wrong with him. Gary felt it in his bones; Neil could see him and Gary knew it was no longer Neil looking back at him from behind those eyes.

Gary watched the mirror frozen in horror as Neil Glixson made his way back to the kitchen. He was no longer showing any signs of worry or concern, rather Neil had a slight knowing snarl creep across his lips as he slowly approached Gary. His hand was still clasping the gun. Gary hopped against hope to wake up and that Neil couldn't actually see him. Neil was just feet away behind Gary when he raised the gun to his own head and walked around to face him. Neil stopped directly in front of him, their eyes locking.

Gary looked past Neil when he noticed something in the mirror behind him, Neil's skull was cracked wide open in the back. Gary tried to scream but no sound would come. He kept thinking "Wake up! Wake up! Wake up!" But that was of no use either. He was locked in. Then a voice, low and raspy crashed through his thoughts coming from whoever was inside Neil's corpse.

"I remember you from the dark."

Gary woke up well before his alarm was set for the evening and he had no desire to go back to sleep. Instead Gary sat down and began penciling his dreams onto his notepad. He stopped once he reached the part where he broke the plot by becoming a character. Gary couldn't use that, it didn't follow any conventional story telling nor did he wish to add himself as the main character into his

WESTING

story. He frankly didn't feel like very many people would want to read about a middle-aged library custodian.

He also was afraid, the dream was still fresh in his mind and he didn't want to dwell on it but it'd felt so vividly real that it was hard not to. That and the fact that he was basing his book on parts of it made it nearly impossible. Gary tried shifting his focus from the end of the dream to the applicable portion for his writing. He needed time to flesh out the project because it definitely needed a central character. Gary thought about using Jonathan Hawley as the lead but doubted anyone would enjoy reading about a devout Christian monk very much either.

Still Gary had to admit; making Jonathan Hawley the focus of a portion of the story would be a good way to tie in Westing's sordid past. Gary figured he'd have to sensationalize and change things anyway, so his obligation to keep in lock step with history was in his mind nil.

"That depends on how you write it." He thought to himself before putting his notebook along with the newly written pages into his bedside dresser, making a mental note to get a fresh ink ribbon when he went out. The work had been easy enough to put to page and it seemed less and less like he'd have to resort to work-shopping the plot as it simply came to him. Gary's fear had mostly subsided as he quickly began getting ready for work, it was just a bad dream. Maybe the next novel would be about something a bit less morbid and his sleep wouldn't be filled with such terrifying visions.

"A comedy for the next project for sure." Gary chuckled.

WESTING

Gary stopped at Sally's again before heading into the library, he'd be damned if he let anyone keep him from his donuts and fresh cream for the night's coffee. "I don't care what anyone tries to say to or about me, I'm not scared and Sally's is the only good part of this entire town." Gary reassured himself staunchly before entering the donut shop but he still dreaded having another incident like the previous days.

Thankfully, there wasn't anyone that Gary recognized this time and he was able to order in peace. Three Boston cream donuts and fresh heavy cream for his coffee to wash them down. "Screw it." He thought. "I'll get fat. I'm an author." Gary smiled to himself as he waited at the counter for his order, happy as could be about the fact that soon he'd be shoving it into his face. His mood had almost shifted entirely until he overheard a conversation that chilled him.

Two older women were sitting in a booth behind him drinking coffee, obviously gossiping.

"Did you hear about Sheriff Trahorn? They found him dead at Herbert's house. Apparently Loren died the other night and he went out on some kind of terrible bender with Herbert… Who they can't find." The older woman said coyly to the other. "I bet he did it. I bet Herbert killed him. That's why they can't find him, he's on the run." The other woman answered. "They always say it's exactly who you think it is."

Gary took his donuts and cream and asked if there was a phone book he could use. "No. Sorry." The man behind the counter answered coldly then went back to his business making fresh dough. Almost everyone in Westing had the same attitude Gary thought, dismal. He knew that the shop had a phone book and it wasn't any trouble for the man to let him look at it. The people of Westing all seemed to have a chip on their shoulder; it was probably from living in that town with all the years of bad luck. Regardless, Gary knew exactly where to find a phone book he could look over and headed to his job at the library. "If they don't want to let me see it I'll just go to the one place in Westing where they pay me to look at books."

Gary was very early to work and he didn't even realize it, in fact he was so early he caught Mrs. Culligan off guard. "Well, I'm glad you're here! I have to leave soon but I'll be in by five AM tomorrow, can't have you on overtime so I'll release you then." She quipped sternly, then rushed to tuck away the small pile of books in her hands out of his sight. Gary recognized one of the titles and his heart began pumping like a jack hammer, it was the library's other book on translating Latin into English; he'd passed it up for the compendium he had taken home because it had seemed less complete.

Gary tried to calm himself, struggling not to show any signs of curiosity or apprehension for fear of what Mrs. Culligan might deduce. He half thought he was losing his mind and quickly decided that he should simply go about his business cleaning the library.

After finishing up the first, then second floors and the lavatories; Gary headed down into the basement. He had decided the day before to haul the books which were too far gone with rot and age out to the dumpster. He'd seen a cellar exit next to the side of the building where the dumpster was located and was hoping it could be opened simply from the inside.

Gary considered himself in luck when he found the

WESTING

lock didn't require a key, glad to avoid Mrs. Culligan for as long as possible. In fact Gary was trying to convince himself not to even think about what may or may not be happening with her at all. "Just do your job. Stop making up crazy scenarios in your head. That's all it is, it's just in your head." Gary told himself calmly, trying to force himself to believe it.

Gary began hauling out the crumbling old volumes to the dumpster. He started with the books, which he could still carry in his arms without getting filthy, throwing them into the dingy bin. Slogging through the water-damaged piles that had sat for god only knows how long on the basement's soggy floor rotting. Gary left the very last of the volumes, which were caked, into the dirty stone for the end, trying desperately to keep his clothes clean. After he'd cleared away the dry portion Gary took a shovel and scrapped up the remainder, little by little clearing the room.

After the floor was cleared away down to the stone for what seemed like the first time in a very long time, Gary resigned himself to his unenviable task of hauling the burnt pile of books out of the corner to the dumpster. On his way to start the job Gary tripped on something, it was something he'd missed while shoveling; an old rusty handle laid into the floor.

Gary bent down and pulled it free of the caked dirt, which had disguised it from him earlier. The metal was extremely rusted as well as exceedingly crudely fashioned, having been shaped long ago by hand hammering. Gary pried the small metal trap door free, revealing an antechamber beneath. The lighting wasn't sufficient for Gary to see the extent of the chamber but what he could make out was an old forge.

"They must have hidden it so no one could discover them melting the gold. What better place to hide it?" Gary was impressed by the discovery and considered descending into the room to explore it further but thought better of it, as he was sure to dirty himself in the process. Instead he closed the trap door carefully so as to not splash muck on his shoes or pants and walked to the last pile of books to deal with, the burnt pile.

The smell coming from the charred volumes was faint but immediately recognizable to Gary, he'd been subjected to it in his dream from the night prior. Determined to put the recollection from his mind, Gary instead contemplated the best way to complete the ordeal as the pile was a considerable distance from the door to the outside of the building.

He decided it was better to shovel them as well, even if the process would take a bit longer. "So it'll take longer. It's not like the old bag has come down to even check in on you, use the shovel and keep your shirt clean."

It didn't seem like a tough call but Gary had worked for his share of slave drivers and knew all too well the price of being caught lagging. He didn't budge; he'd use the shovel regardless of how much extra time it took. Mrs. Culligan would be the first to yell at him about an unclean work outfit he reminded himself. "Just get to it, the longer you wait the longer it'll take."

As Gary painstakingly cleared away the mound of charred books, scooping them onto the small shovel and walking them to the dumpster outside, he noticed one of them wasn't a new edition like the

WESTING

others. Upon further inspection Gary saw that the volume seemed to be in the same hand as the journal of brother Jonathan Hawley.

Gary picked the book up from the floor; it was charred in a large spot that ran in a single line across the front. However, on the back of the book there were four indented deep burns that Gary immediately recognized as the indentations of four fingers. He recoiled and dropped the book on the small table next to the stairwell leading back up to the first floor. This must have been the book the previous librarian was holding when she died.

Outside Gary could hear the rumble of thunder and through the open metal cellar doors he could see flashes of lightning crackling across the sky overhead. Within no time at all the first lonely droplets became sheets of rain, blanketing everything in their frigid grasp. Mist rose up from the valley and began creeping into the deserted parking lot.

Gary had the feeling that the storm rolling in was no accident. He felt like it'd been summoned. "Stop thinking everything is magically connected, you're not being rational." Gary tried convincing himself that he'd been irrationally paranoid all day, first by imagining the gossiping women to be using the names of people he'd dreamt up; then by assuming that Mrs. Culligan's reading interest had something to do with all of his delusional fantasies of secret treasures.

Now his automatic assumption that the burnt books he'd found stacked in the basement corner had anything to do with the prior librarian's death and finally somehow making the connection of an oncoming storm to some kind of magical occurrence. "It's just a storm old boy, sometimes you let your imagination get the best of you."

Gary tried to chuckle to himself as he went over to close the rusty metal cellar door, even going so far as to joke with himself audibly. "You really are too caught up in your stories." His mother had always scolded him for having his head in the clouds dreaming up far off lands and unknown riches, great adventures and world saving feats. His father never put him down and wouldn't let her utter a word to Gary in malice in his presence. Try as he might to take his mind off of the many eerie connections Gary had made that day, he simply couldn't. Not in his heart. In his heart Gary was scared. Gary was scared out of his mind.

It felt like he was being watched every minute he

was in that old library.

Hunted even.

Gary closed the basements folding metal doors and latched them, locking them then tapping three times on the metal to reassure himself he'd done it.

Tap.

Tap.

Tap.

Gary then made his way back across the room to the stairwell leading upstairs, reluctantly taking the charred book from it's place on the table before heading up. Gary attempted not to touch the burnt portions, because as much as he tried not to; all he saw when he looked at it was the seared impression of a hand.

Tap.

Tap.

Tap.

Gary locked the basement stairwell door behind him and quickly tapped his key thrice, making his way to sit down at the desk and look for the phone book; at least to put his mind at ease. He rummaged through the desk drawers until he found it but it did little to assuage his fears, for within it's pages printed as plain as day were their names.

All of them.

Herbert Scaghill.

Loren Scaghill.

Jeremiah Trahorn.

Neil Glixson.

WESTING

Betty and Jim Linkler.

Gary was terrified. So much so that when Mrs. Culligan stormed out of her office and strutted out the front door he nearly jumped out of his seat. Luckily she was in far too big of a rush to notice. She didn't even say goodbye to Gary and he saw she didn't lock up her office or the front door on her way out.

Gary waited at the desk expecting her to rush back in at any moment but she didn't. Mrs. Culligan had looked as though there wasn't anything in the world Gary could have said to call her back into the building that would have mattered, she seemed determined to leave but to what end he couldn't be sure.

Gary opened the desk and was about to return the phone book to it's place when he noticed two time cards with the names Bartlett Cobb and Murray Sax sitting on the bottom of the drawer.

"I hear Bartlett and Murray both quit the night it happened. Maybe they had something to do with it?" The phrase relayed in Gary's mind. He'd heard it outside the mayor's office the day of his interview but hadn't thought of it since.

Gary Looked up Murray Sax in the phone book and called the number. The line rang for what seemed like an eternity and Gary was about to hang up when a woman answered, her voice shaky as if she'd been crying. "Hello?" She asked less than hopefully. "Hello is Murray in?" Gary asked as politely as possible.

There was a deep exhale on the other line as the woman struggled to compose herself. "No. He hasn't been home in days now. This is his wife. Can I take a message? You haven't perchance seen him?" She was on the verge of weeping and Gary could tell from the tone of her voice that she never expected to give Murray whatever message he might leave. Gary apologized for any inconvenience and said he'd call back another time, then promptly hung up.

Gary thought about his dream and the man who he had followed into the abandoned mineshaft. Shivers coursed through his body. It was getting impossibly hard for Gary to ignore the fact that whatever was going on was connected to his dreams. First the names being in the phone book, now the crying wife of Murray Sax.

Gary opened the phone book back up and searched until he found Bartlett Cobb, unwilling to accept the logic that his own dreams had been happening in reality. He took the phone off the hook and dialed his number. After a few rings a gruff sounding man picked up. "Hello?" The man who Gary assumed to be Bartlett asked. "Is this Mr. Bartlett Cobb?" Gary politely inquired. "Yeah, what's this regarding?" Gary cleared his throat before answering. "Is this the same Bartlett Cobb who used to work at the Westing library?" The line went silent.

"Hello?" Gary blurted out after a long pause.

"You the guy that took the job?" Bartlett coldly asked.

WESTING

"Yeah. I was just wondering…" Before Gary could utter another word Bartlett cut him off. "Quit."

The line went dead.

Gary tried calling back but the line was busy and in his heart he knew the man had taken it off the hook. Gary hung up the phone and went to put back the phone book in the desk drawer when he noticed a key that read "Office" at the bottom of it. He laughed to himself, Mrs. Culligan certainly didn't know about the key. Not that she'd remembered to lock her office anyway, Gary was almost sure of it.

Gary walked over to her door and tried the knob. He was correct, the door had been left unlocked and Gary could simply push the door open. But he didn't. Gary used his newfound key to lock the door, then went back to his desk. He still didn't want to be fired on the spot.

Gary knew in the back of his mind there was a good chance that everything was somehow just a coincidence or a concoction of his imagination. Gary trusted his sanity less after the day he couldn't account for while on LSD. Sure, it may have been all a hallucination and Gary had actually never left his spot in front of his fire the entire time but there was more than a little doubt in his mind. The memory of the faces surrounding him was so vivid and haunting and the following day lost in the woods felt nightmarishly real.

Gary looked down at his hand, he'd unconsciously scrawled something on the open notepad laid upon the desktop while thinking things out.

WESTING

"Culligan's dead. She's with Neil Glixson."

He didn't remember writing it. Gary took the paper, ripping it out of the notepad and putting it into his bag, first scrawling over the phrase until it was completely obscured by the black ink. In the pit of his stomach Gary knew the statement to be true. It was the gold she had been after.

Everything felt very wrong.

Gary's stomach was in knots and he couldn't shake the feeling of dread that had fallen over him. He felt like someone was watching him from between the darkened rows off in the library behind him. Gary turned around to face the space, shining his flashlight around to illuminate it but finding nothing out of place.

Still Gary felt uneasy and decided that he wasn't going to leave the lights off that night, regardless of what Mrs. Culligan might say; so he got up from the desk and turned them on. The fluorescents hummed dully for a minute then blinked on slowly. Gary put a pot of water for coffee onto the small portable burner and put a new filter in the top, pouring in his idea of the perfect amount of grounds. "Most people put too much in and it tastes bitter, even with cream and sugar."

Ka-boom!!!

Lightning flashed through the blackened sky outside, the storm was pounding harder than ever. The loud crash of it striking not too far off was quickly followed by the earth-shaking boom of more thunder, which rattled the books in their shelves.

Gary was ok with ignoring his suspicions, reasoning that even if his wild fears were true he wanted nothing more to do with finding out. Maybe he was just having a delayed manic reaction to his entire life's complete disenfranchisement now that he was in a position to actually process his emotions, no longer purely running on survival instincts and denial.

"Well at least I have good coffee and I'm not out in the rain. It'll all be ok. I just have to do my job and that's it. Do your work, mind your business, enjoy what life gives you and be grateful for it." Gary dumped the now steaming hot water into the top of the percolator and smelled the wonderful aroma that wafted off the freshly brewing beans.

That's when again he heard something mixed with the thunder rumbling outside. Something soft but distinctive. Something definitely not outside the building. It sounded like a woman faintly sobbing from upstairs.

Gary tried to brush it off but he couldn't. He'd heard it. There wasn't a doubt in his mind. There also wasn't a chance that Gary was about to go investigate what the source of it was. Gary had another idea, one that involved him getting into Mrs. Culligan's office. He decided that he had to wait until morning until Mrs. Culligan was due in. Then he could look into her face and put aside the thoughts that what he had dismissed as just an unconscious doodle was truer than any of the works of fiction in the rows behind him.

WESTING

Or, if something terrifying he'd only known in his worst nightmares was actually unfolding in real life. For the first time Gary hoped Mrs. Culligan would storm through the front door and reprimanded him for leaving the lights on.

If she'd simply walked through the door he'd know his fantasies were just that. If she didn't he was going into her office for answers. Gary had strong suspicions that there were papers in the office that were from Jonathan Hawley's journal or at least something pertaining to whatever it was that caused so many deaths in the town of Westing. Something otherworldly that Gary was growing increasingly convinced was real.

Gary did indeed also question his own sanity and

tried not to let anything break him. "It may or may not be real but either way I'm not going to risk losing my job. I love my kids too much. Get a hold of yourself. You've come too far. Look at the facts. Until she doesn't show up tomorrow morning you know more than likely this is you just not sleeping long enough and maybe having spent too many years on the bottle.

Or the drugs.

You're tired; you've been having terrible dreams. Your sleep schedule is off. You miss the kids. Just sit down and wait like you're supposed to. When Mrs. Culligan comes in the morning you can go home and sleep. Then you'll make sense of all of this." He reassured himself but still he wasn't able to calm his nerves.

WESTING

It was all real. He felt it in his bones.

If it was he didn't know what he'd do. Gary kept running through the scenarios. Leaving town was the only one that made any sense. Leave town and fast. That was the only thing he could think to do that would allow himself to get free of the nightmare. Of course there was a tiny voice in his head wondering about the gold. Gary knew he should ignore it. He also knew that amount of gold would be worth a fortune.

A fortune that would change his life.

Gary sat put. The storm raging around him in the night keeping him company, he pulled out the book he'd borrowed for translating Latin to English and got to work transcribing the second journal by Jonathan Hawley. This journal was an account of the mysterious female traveler whom the party of men from his flock had found in the woods the evening they'd made camp returning from their barter. She'd looked disheveled, emaciated and confused. A young, beautiful woman dressed in ragged puritan clothing who couldn't remember who she was or where she'd come from.

The only thing she'd kept repeating was about people she'd seen following her in the dark.

The men brought the young woman into the colony and to the three leaders of the settlement. At first Jonathan, Levi and Abernathy had all agreed that the woman should be given safe haven from the wilderness and time to awaken from whatever had taken her memory. What a horrid plight Gary thought, to be truly lost without memories to know who one was but enough wits to know how to behave and even speak. Jonathan had taken pity on the poor woman, her mind gone blank; leaving her to wonder aloud who she was and why she couldn't remember.

That was before the wayward woman discovered the hidden gold on accident, perhaps it was the lords way of punishing him brother Hawley mused; contemplating her true purpose.

She had gone into the streets of Westing and began talking of what she'd seen before Levi and Abernathy got ahold of her. They proposed she was a witch to the rest of the congregation; a majority were dimwitted and desperate enough to believe them. Jonathan himself had hidden the treasure in the basement of his home, in a secret room under his floorboards.

When the people of Westing found no evidence of her claims the lost traveler's fate was sealed. The congregation saw her burn alive after what Levi and Abernathy claimed was a fair trial. Little did the people of Westing know Levi and Abernathy had tormented her in the attic of the church for days to get a confession.

They'd found the poor woman guilty of being a witch and as soon as the verdict was levied she burst into flames of her own accord. The immolation had consumed most of the churches upper floors but the building had been saved by a storm, which rolled in off the mountains. In her dying moments the woman cursed the people of Westing and their treasure, condemning any who were part of the congregation or their descendants that ever laid a hand upon it. Knowing that a hunger would be in the gut of every person in the town of Westing for it from that moment on.

Brother Jonathan Hawley wrote that he knew no amount of prayers or penance would absolve them, that he'd seen it in the eyes of the dying woman as the flames consumed her. For their sins they had been doomed. The lost traveler was indeed a witch, a servant of darkness sent to test their faith; they'd failed.

"Ahuh… huh…"

Gary put down the book. He'd heard it clearly this time, hushed sobbing muddled under the rain echoing from the floors above him. Gary had made out a raspy-hollowed-out voice. It said his name in the softest whisper, just barely audible above the sounds of the storm.

"Gary…"

Gary sat still. He was determined not to give in. To not let fear overcome him or to allow himself to admit what he'd heard was real. It sounds absurd when your life and livelihood aren't on the line to judge someone for their seemingly ludicrous justifications. But each person has different mental ways of coping with the unknown and Gary had already experienced a drug-fueled trauma that made him question the validity of the disembodied voice.

He almost had himself convinced again when the lightning struck the power line just outside the library, knocking the power out. In the flash Gary saw a reflection in the glass just behind him. Two eyes shining through the murky blackness. He grabbed for his flashlight in the dark, wheeling around as soon as his fingers wrapped around it. He clicked it on, then grabbed the bat from underneath the desk.

No one was there.

He picked up the phone but it was dead. After slamming it down Gary decided that he didn't care if he was scolded or fired he was going to go to his car. He wasn't about to stay another minute in that library, Gary made up his mind that regardless of the ramifications he'd wait out the rest of his shift in his car.

"I'll come up with an excuse for the old bag when I'm outside." Gary ran to the door and then headed out. Tapping three times after locking the door behind him.

Tap.

Tap.

Tap.

Silly as it might be he not only wanted to make sure the door was locked for Mrs. Culligan when she arrived, he wanted to keep whoever or whatever he'd seen inside. After the last tap of his keys hit the aging wood Gary went racing across the parking lot towards the safety of his car. The vehicle Gary spent many nights in alone. He was halfway to it when he distinctly heard a sound, even through the storm. The three bangs on the front door.

Bang!

BANG!!!

BANG!!!!!

Gary didn't turn around to look, he could feel the eyes on him coming from the darkness within. He piled into his car which blessedly was completely fogged up from the freezing rain. Gary thought about turning on the heat but didn't out of fear of clearing the windows.

He simply sat there shivering, wet and freezing in the October night, wishing he could simply leave but knowing he couldn't. Knowing that if he did he would risk sleeping in his car every night again possibly from then on. He came up with excuses that he'd tell Mrs. Culligan when she returned in the morning, maybe a story about how cold he'd been inside with the power off. Gary figured that sounded reasonable, as it wasn't very warm in the building even with the heat on. "It's not as if I'd be abandoning the place." Gary pondered.

Gary knew that to keep warm, all he had to do was get the blanket out of the trunk and wrap himself in it. It was thick and had kept him toasty on even the coldest of nights. He didn't even need to go back outside to do so, he could pull it through the cars backseat from the trunk as part of the seat flipped down and gave him access to it.

Gary crawled into the back, taking his wet shoes off out of habit so he didn't mess up the upholstery. He then pulled up the handle releasing the locking mechanism, swinging the seat down and exposing the blanket. Gary pulled it out and began curling the blanket around himself when he saw it, the charred face smiling at him from the back of the trunk. Gary slammed the seat back into place, wedging himself against it.

Bang!

BANG!!!

BANG!!!!!

The upholstery bulged as the backseat rattled from the impacts, Gary used every ounce of his strength to keep it in place.

"Go away!!!" Gary screamed, then he felt the car shake; as if someone was getting out of the trunk.

"KA-BOOM!!!"

Gary heard the slam as the trunk swung shut hard. Then saw a finger touch the glass of the window overlooking his hideaway in the back seat. The wide eyes peering into the car we're looking straight at him. Gary darted under the blanket, pulling it up over

WESTING

his head.

"It's not real." Gary kept telling himself. Unable to move or peek out for fear of what he might see, tucked away like a child under the heavy wool.

"Just don't look. Just don't look. Just don't look…"

Gary heard the front lock pop and the sound of the door opening, then for a long while all he heard was the storm.

Gary lay motionless, listening to the rain pelt the front seat and feeling the dampness spilling onto his legs under the blanket. Gary didn't dare move, keeping his eyes pressed tightly shut against the woolen cloth.

Gary stayed that way for hours, until his feet were so cold he'd lost feeling in them and they were beginning to throb. The entire time he'd felt as though there was someone hovering just over him, he could even hear them breathing. There also was the terrible smell of seared necrotic death, more pungent than even in his dream.

Gary imagined the face he'd seen in his nightmare, lurking in the darkness of the basement stairs at Neil Glixson's; it had been the same face that was glaring back at him from the trunk. Burnt and ravenous, it's eyes and teeth accentuated through the loss of skin. He imagined those knowing eyes looking through the woolen blanket right past his closed eyelids and into his very soul.

WESTING

"It's just a flashback, please don't lose this job over taking that garbage." Gary tried to muster his courage to pull the blanket from his face and look but he simply could not. His mind was petrified with fear, real or an after effect of the hallucinogenic drug he'd ingested; Gary's limbs refused to move.

"If that old bag pulls in to this parking lot and finds you like this you're toast. Please Gary, please for once in your life don't ruin everything!" Gary got up fast, ripping the blanket off and hopping up off the seat on pure adrenaline; ready to fight for his life. The car was empty; the driver's door lay open to the predawn parking lot; the rain still steadily falling.

Although, the smell of burnt hair and flesh still lingered in the car.

Gary slowly scanned around him through the now defrosted windows into the dwindling night. Not finding anything around the car he reached over the front seat and quickly shut the door, slamming it then locking it. Gary tried to calm himself and decided to turn on the car to get warm, his legs and the wool blanket were soaked and Gary knew that unless he warmed up he'd surely catch a cold if he hadn't already. He climbed into the passenger seat and put the heat on full blast.

The sun was slowly coming up and Gary's legs were no longer throbbing from the pain of the cold. Somehow he'd made it through the dark hours. He was certain that in no time he would see Mrs. Culligan come driving into the parking lot, furious that he wasn't at his post. Certain that what had happened the night prior wasn't real. The rain had all but stopped, and the sky began turning golden and violet hues behind the last of the black and grey storm clouds. Gary turned the car off and got out, stepping into the fresh morning air and stretching his legs.

He felt silly.

The brisk misty morning air hung with the fresh smells of the fall countryside and Gary all but screamed at himself for being such a fool. "Don't be so hard on yourself. Be proud of yourself for not leaving and for standing up to your fears." Gary had made up his mind that the worst was over and in a way the dawn seemed to signify that.

Gary locked up his car after spreading his blanket over the wet front seat so that maybe he wouldn't soak his trousers when he came back to drive himself home. He walked confidently to the front door and unlocked it, stepping back into the still darkened building.

Gary assumed that the power wouldn't be back on for some time but he also had remembered the three donuts he'd left untouched on the desk. The coffee maker wouldn't work without electricity but Gary didn't mind eating the confections with a cup of the cold black leftovers from the night before. He just was grateful to have the meal.

He took the donuts and coffee and went outside to sit and wait for Mrs. Culligan. The library still felt a bit eerie to him in the dark with all the power off, sunlight or not. And so Gary posted up on the front bench just outside the door, polishing off the donuts and strong brew quickly as the sky cleared overhead and the birds chirped to their hearts content but Mrs.

WESTING

Culligan never showed. Nor did any cars go past Gary on the road into town, or out of it.

The morning drug on into the afternoon and Gary knew something was terribly wrong. Reluctantly he made his way back inside. Gary would be fired on the spot if Mrs. Culligan came and found him in her office, of that he had no doubts but he no longer cared. He took the key and opened the lock, pushing the door open all the way this time.

"Be quick, in and out. Don't touch anything you can't put back exactly, she'll know if anything is moved." Gary thought to himself and in his head he answered. "No she won't. She's dead." Gary tried to quiet the thought as he walked swiftly to the desk and opened the bottom drawer, the one he'd seen Mrs. Culligan hide something from him in.

Within it Gary saw something it took all his will not to run from. A single, very old, gold coin lying perched on top of the missing pages from Jonathan Hawley's journal. Gary's heart was pounding out of his chest as he reached down and retrieved the pile. Only making matters worse was what Gary found lying underneath. There, written in what Gary could identify as Mrs. Culligan's hand were notes on the deaths of Neil Glixson, sheriff Jeremiah Trahorn, Betty and Jim Linkler and Herbert and Loren Scaghill with his name written underneath followed by the chilling accompanying description: "He knows something. Keep watching. Don't trust him."

Gary almost lost his nerve, looking around to see if anyone could possibly be lurking anywhere nearby to observe him. After putting everything back into the desk and heading out of the office Gary attempted to convince himself everything was a test and he'd failed. However after a few more hours dragged on Gary went back into the office and this time stayed there until he'd completely copied the journal pages. The entire time Gary neither heard any cars pass nor saw anyone on the road outside which he periodically hawked.

After completing his transcription Gary put everything back in it's place and locked the Drawer. It was now late afternoon and he was beginning to feel the pull of exhaustion as well as pangs of terrified worry. Something was deadly wrong, of that Gary was sure. He tried the phone one more time but the line was still dead. He'd have to lock the place up and head down to the mayor's office in town to let someone know the situation. Gary felt hesitant to leave the library without anyone to watch it but he also more than anything wanted answers as to the whereabouts of Mrs. Culligan.

Gary made sure all the entrances were locked, simply pulling on both the front and basement doors instead of tapping with his key this time. Gary didn't even take all of his things with him out of the library, expecting that he'd more than likely be right back if Mrs. Culligan couldn't be located to stand guard until she could be found; or until someone else could stand watch.

He barely looked up from the ground in front of himself on the way over to his car. And although the storm had past, Gary felt as if there was still an electric charge in the air. He was on edge as he wheeled out of the otherwise empty parking lot, an unease that only grew as he made his way down the deserted road into town.

CHAPTER SIX: NO ONE KNOWS WHAT WAITS FOR THEM AT THE END OF THE ROAD.

Westing was a ghost town. None of the streets had any sign of life on them, not even a vagrant or a single old lady; of which Westing held an abundance. Gary also noted none of the stores were opened, when he drove by Sally's even it's doors were closed and it's lights off. The neon 24/7 sign conspicuously dark.

Gary had waves of paranoia wash over him. He really began to question his own sanity when he pulled up to the town hall and it too was completely devoid of any signs of life. Gary pulled over to see if anyone was inside but there wasn't. The doors were locked and after several minutes of loudly banging on them Gary gave up.

There was no signs of anyone. Even the birds were no longer chirping. As a matter of fact Gary noticed that it was quiet enough that he could hear himself breathing. Gary noticed something else, as he looked up the road he spotted what was the exact home from his dream on the outskirts of town. The large home of Neil Glixson sitting atop of the hill, surrounded by large well-trimmed hedges.

A fire hydrant exploded at the far end of the road to Gary's left sending it's caps hurling hundreds of feet into the air as cascades of water sprayed high into the heavens. Not knowing what to make of any of it Gary got back into his car and drove towards the

WESTING

house, his nerves telling him to simply leave town immediately but his curiosity outweighing every other impulse.

The next thing Gary noticed that was completely out of place was a car smashed into the side of a home. It looked like no one had attended to it yet as the engine was still audibly running and it's tail lights were still on but there was no signs of the driver, or home owner, or of anyone else. Only a thick coating of soot within the vehicle and the now all-too-familiar acrid aroma.

He knew he should turn back but he couldn't. Gary couldn't stop what was drawing him onward; it was curiosity; curiosity and greed. The barren streets screamed something is terribly wrong here and everywhere he looked Gary spotted little things, which unsettled him. A woman's purse and shoe sitting discarded on the sidewalk. A dog running away from him with his leash dragging behind. Bags of groceries left unattended inside the open trunk of a car.

"Where is everyone?" Gary murmured to himself as he scuttled out of his once compact mobile home onto the street in front of Neil Glixson's mansion. That's when Gary noticed Mrs. Culligan's unmistakable old grey Buick station wagon with its freshly polished chrome parked in the driveway around the back of the house, it'd been pulled in as far as possible so as to be hidden from the street. "Just go in and take a look to see if the gold is really there, then leave." Walking up to the home past the hedges took courage for Gary, especially since he'd recently seen them in a dream from above.

There was also the specter of unspeakable horror

WESTING

potentially laying in wait.

"Do it, walk up to the door Gary." He forced his feet to take one step at a time towards the lavish mansion, each more filled with dread.

Gary reached the front door but had to convince himself to open it. "It's upstairs under the bed. Just walk into the house and get it. Then you can leave this town and never come back. Take it to Neil's pawnshop connection; pretend Neil hired you to make the switch. You'll be set for life. Just turn the handle and go inside." Gary mustered up enough courage that he was able to open the door and walk in. Sure enough there was blood sprayed all over the kitchen and there was a bullet hole in the wall.

Neil Glixson however was nowhere to be found,

although his gun was on the floor next to a puddle of blood. Gary almost tripped on it as he hurried out of the kitchen, making his way past the basement door, which was closed. He tried to hurry, not wanting to spend another second more than necessary. His footsteps resounded off the creaky wooden stairs as he hustled up them, the only sound beyond distant barking. Once at the top Gary went right into Neil's bedroom and pulled his travel bags out from where they'd been hidden under the mattress.

Gary could feel the sheer weight of them in his grasp, hearing the coins clink together as he freed the over stuffed bags from their hiding spot. Gary quickly unzipped a corner, making sure the contents were as he suspected. It was indeed filled to almost bursting with old gold coins, which perfectly matched the one he'd found in Mrs. Culligan's desk. As soon had he seen it's contents Gary zipped the case closed and made his way down the steps carrying the heavy bags, the coins making a racket no matter how steady he tried to hold them.

As he reached the bottom of the stairs Gary paused.

He knew someone was in the house, there was the noxious smell of fire hanging in the air and the door to the basement was now open.

Gary listened, trying to stay as still as possible.

He could hear someone breathing.

"Gary…" The muted cackle rang in his ears coming from the depths of the basement, no louder than a hushed murmur.

Gary made his way towards the kitchen door in a mad dash, running as swiftly as he could. He was almost to it when he saw it in the reflection of the mirror. The countless dead eyes peering out at him from the darkness of the basement stairs.

"We'll be waiting for you." The cracking cackle whispered, a sea of voices crushed into a single dissonant tone. Gary didn't hesitate to run to his car, he wasn't even looking by the time the fire made it's way out of the depths.

The house was quickly engulfed in towering flames as Gary floored it down the hill and off towards the main road. By the time he passed Sally's the town of Westing was racing him into the earth as the coal vein it was built upon reached a fully blazing inferno

WESTING

underneath it, collapsing it into it's depths.

Gary just made it out with his life.

His life and a fortune in gold.

Gary didn't bother going back to the library instead he drove away from the burning crater where Westing once stood, the forbidden treasure resting in the backseat of his beat up old sedan; a fresh start for a man many had long ago written off.

That night Gary met up with George McCullen who was three sheets to the wind drunk waiting for Neil Glixson with the cash. Gary simply told him Neil sent him and handed over the treasure. George wasn't in any condition to care about anything more than the bags of gold Gary laid out before him. He took Gary's story at face value about Neil sending him to collect the money, handing Gary his half of the two million in crisp one hundred dollar bills, no questions asked.

Gary couldn't believe how easy it had been and counted the cash twice on his drive over to the bed and breakfast he'd booked himself just down the street from his old house. He knew the couple were looking to sell the place, which hadn't meant much more to him than a day dream up until that point but circumstances had changed. The memories of Westing buried just as deep as the town itself within the recesses of his mind, a bad dream to be forgotten until the very end of his life.

As Gary pulled into the quaint old cottage's long

gravel driveway, he knew he was home.

AFTERWARD:

When the catastrophic aftermath was discovered the local government officials scrubbed the town of Westing off of the map. After the Centralia disaster in 1962 they'd learned that keeping such ecological hazards out of the news was easier than dealing with people trying to go into the location.

They closed off the main road in and out of town, then covered the first stretch off the highway over with hundreds of trees so that nature quickly reclaimed the space. The only remaining way in or out of Westing left was the access road located behind the library and that too was chained off from the general public. Even if someone had wanted to drive into the town proper they couldn't because it no longer existed.

It was a burning chasm.

There is now no mention of the town in any official records or maps as it's neighbors don't want outsiders coming in to explore the area. The risk of the potential intruders getting lost in the now densely overgrown brush, which is prone to catching fire or to giving way to the smoldering caverns below is far too great.

It's something that has been a constant problem for the town of Centralia, which experienced a similar event involving another underground coal vein fire.

WESTING

Unlike the tragedy in Westing it made the national news before the authorities could get a lid on it.

Westing was different; the town wasn't even missed except by a few truckers and one or two folks who had family there. These weren't people who were concerned with going to the lengths to even find out what happened to their kin or the town. Most of the inhabitants of Westing by the time of it's demise had been all but abandoned there.

The only investigation that was conducted into what transpired in the town of Westing concluded very quickly. It deduced that the victims of the tragedy were killed by the massive underground coal vein inferno collapsing the town into its belly. The area was and still is considered to be actively burning and is expected to do so for hundreds of years, making any investigation into the individual disappearances impossible.

One discovery that did lead to a small police inquiry was made by a group of teens that illegally backpacked into the site almost four decades later. It was Gary Wettle's rough manuscript and two much older books, tucked away in the dresser drawer next to his bedside in one of the few remaining buildings outlying the town proper. After a good deal of debate as to what they should do with it, the teens begrudgingly brought the manuscript and volumes to the police.

However the manuscript as well as the teens testimony was panned off by the officers almost immediately as most likely being a hoax of the youngsters invention, or the morbid prank of some other equally untrustworthy trespasser. It wasn't until three years later when the old library was being

WESTING

stripped for salvage by the county that anything further was suspected.

Because of it's location on the ridge outside of Westing, the library was deemed safe enough for the county to scrap out for profit by the local officials as it stood far enough from the burning sink hole and it's contents were valuable enough to risk the hazards. A condo for each of the three county commissioners after promises of new job creation was certainly a justification. It was during the ransacking of the building that some additional odd things were uncovered and Gary Wettle was sought for questioning. By that time Gary Wettle wasn't around to answer.

The police re-examined the manuscript and books as well as the few pieces newly discovered evidence; an impression left on a note pad, one gold coin and some pages from one of the journals found in Gary Wettle's nightstand. In the end the case was again closed, being written off as nothing more than fictional work and coincidence. Though the investigation did find a few very odd corroborating pieces of evidence and a historical mystery.

One such discovery came in the form of the long picked clean skeleton belonging to Herbert Skaghill. The body was found up on the bluffs that were once referred to as honeymoon cut or lover's point, with a bullet hole through the skull. Again it was assumed that Gary had overheard the news of the tragedy and integrated it into his writing but as he was missing there wasn't anything to be done but assume.

Another thing was unearthed upon examining the basement of the old library and uncovering the hidden forge. Buried in the ground just shallow enough to be protruding from it's depths were four unknown sets of human remains who's carbon dating placed them somewhere in the late 1600's. It has been theorized by many that they are the remains of the missing town leaders and the unjustly murdered lost traveler.

All four remains showed signs of having been burned.

There were a few detectives who thought it was strange how many of the writings that had been discovered of Mr. Wettle's were specifically about actual residents of Westing, not to mention it's rumored treasure. Even moreover since Gary Wettle had lived a very rich life and died with a sizable estate after leaving the town as the only survivor of the disaster.

His fortune was indeed quite vast, including some very expensive books from within his own personal library. A library which had been built as an addition to the already large converted bed and breakfast he had purchased in cold hard cash. Gary Wettle had a habit of buying things in that manner. He had acquired several properties this way in the neighborhood, a home for his father and each of his children.

Gary's relationship with his father included involving the old man in his book keeping for his many business ventures, they were closer than ever during their remaining years and many pointed to that as the reason for Gary's great prosperity. In the end, all the detectives could really debate was the success of his writings and speculate that maybe he'd been padding the numbers of his book sales.

WESTING

Indeed Gary Wettle had been a self-published entrepreneur, never signing another outside contract of any kind. Gary also was something of an established book trader, his love of rare volumes and funds to procure them were no secret to anyone who'd known him. How he had become so widely distributed was something of a mystery, the publishing source of his books was later revealed to be a shell company but because of Mr. Wettle's vanishment nothing was ever further scrutinized.

Either way most who met or knew of Gary Wettle, including the detectives assigned his case, envied the life he'd led and wished that even if it was within the pages of his will; he'd written just one hint as to what really happened to the town of Westing. However Gary hadn't written a single horror story or morbid tale since leaving that place, all of his subsequent works were either adventure novels or children's books.

Gary Wettle had indeed seen enough horror for one lifetime.

The last anyone ever saw or heard from Mr. Wettle was his son Caleb when he told him that he was going to go camping on his own one warm October evening, that he'd be back after the weekend so he shouldn't worry and that he loved him very much.

Caleb Wettle knew his father too well to not suspect that something was wrong but there wasn't much he could do. His father had always been a strong willed man but Caleb had never known him to go camping or even stay in a hotel without room service once they could afford it. Their entire childhood after he bought the giant old house down the street had been

WESTING

first class all the way. They'd all traveled the globe promoting his father's writings, but never once when they could help it had they ever even stayed in anywhere Caleb didn't consider luxurious. So on Monday evening when he hadn't heard from his father, Caleb called the police.

A weeklong search of the local campgrounds around Gary's property yielded nothing and volunteers were called off. Three years went by and the case went cold, Gary was considered missing without a trace. His son did find a will as well as a letter left for him and his sister, neither mentioned anything to do with his disappearance; just that he loved them and was proud of them and grateful for the life he'd gotten to live with them.

That they were his greatest achievements and most priceless treasures.

ADAM AHLBRANDT

When Gary Wettle's secluded campsite was discovered it had been completely by chance and on accident. It was located on a man's property who claimed to have been an old acquaintance, tucked away on a road no one ever used. The site was stocked with plenty of firewood and an untouched cooler filled with the rancid remnants of hot dogs and eggs. Gary's favorite coffee mug was found next to a fold out chair, sitting empty in front of a long disused fire pit. His body was never recovered.

The End.